"What have you done to me, Virginia?" asked the Duke. *"Why should I feel like this?"*

"You are imagining it," she responded, her voice low and frightened.

"How easy if I could dismiss it as something I have imagined," he said. "But love at first sight does exist in the world. It has happened to me!"

"I wonder what you mean by love?" Virginia asked.

"I mean," the Duke replied, "that it is love when you know you have found the other half of yourself, the person to whom you belong and who belongs to you."

He had not attempted to touch her, and yet Virginia felt as if he held her against him . . .

Books by Barbara Cartland

- THE ADVENTURER
- AGAIN THIS RAPTURE
- ARMOUR AGAINST LOVE
- THE AUDACIOUS ADVENTURESS
- BARBARA CARTLAND'S BOOK OF BEAUTY AND HEALTH
- THE BITTER WINDS OF LOVE
- BLUE HEATHER
- BROKEN BARRIERS
- THE CAPTIVE HEART
- THE COIN OF LOVE
- THE COMPLACENT WIFE
- CUPID RIDES PILLION
- DANCE ON MY HEART
- DESIRE OF THE HEART
- THE DREAM WITHIN
- DESPERATE DEFIANCE
- A DUEL OF HEARTS
- ELIZABETH EMPRESS OF AUSTRIA
- ELIZABETH IN LOVE
- THE ENCHANTING EVIL
- THE ENCHANTED MOMENT
- THE ENCHANTED WALTZ
- ESCAPE FROM PASSION
- A GHOST IN MONTE CARLO
- THE GOLDEN GONDOLA
- A HALO FOR THE DEVIL
- A HAZARD OF HEARTS
- A HEART IS BROKEN
- THE HIDDEN EVIL
- THE HIDDEN HEART
- THE HORIZONS OF LOVE
- THE IRRESISTIBLE BUCK
- JOSEPHINE EMPRESS OF FRANCE
- THE KISS OF THE DEVIL
- THE KISS OF PARIS
- A KISS OF SILK
- THE KNAVE OF HEARTS
- THE LEAPING FLAME
- LIGHTS OF LOVE
- A LIGHT TO THE HEART
- THE LITTLE PRETENDER
- LOST ENCHANTMENT
- LOST LOVE
- LOVE AND LINDA
- LOVE AT FORTY
- LOVE FORBIDDEN
- LOVE HOLDS THE CARDS
- LOVE IN HIDING
- LOVE IN PITY
- LOVE IS AN EAGLE
- LOVE IS CONTRABAND
- LOVE IS DANGEROUS
- LOVE IS THE ENEMY
- LOVE IS MINE
- LOVE ME FOREVER
- LOVE ON THE RUN
- LOVE TO THE RESCUE
- LOVE UNDER FIRE
- THE MAGIC OF HONEY
- MESSENGER OF LOVE
- METTERNICH THE PASSIONATE DIPLOMAT
- MONEY, MAGIC AND MARRIAGE
- NO HEART IS FREE
- THE ODIOUS DUKE
- OPEN WINGS
- OUT OF REACH
- PASSIONATE PILGRIM
- THE PRETTY HORSE-BREAKERS
- THE PRICE IS LOVE
- A RAINBOW TO HEAVEN
- THE RELUCTANT BRIDE
- THE RUNAWAY HEART
- THE SCANDALOUS LIFE OF KING CAROL
- THE SECRET FEAR
- THE SMUGGLED HEART
- A SONG OF LOVE
- STARS IN MY HEART
- STOLEN HALO
- SWEET ADVENTURE
- SWEET ENCHANTRESS
- SWEET PUNISHMENT
- THIEF OF A HEART
- THE THIEF OF LOVE
- THIS TIME IT'S LOVE
- TOWARDS THE STARS
- THE UNKNOWN HEART
- THE UNPREDICTABLE BRIDE
- A VIRGIN IN MAYFAIR
- A VIRGIN IN PARIS
- WE DANCED ALL NIGHT
- WHERE IS LOVE
- THE WINGS OF LOVE
- WINGS ON MY HEART
- WOMAN THE ENIGMA

11
THE UNKNOWN HEART

A JOVE BOOK

Copyright © 1969 by Barbara Cartland

All rights reserved. No part of this publication may be reproduced or transmitted in any form or by any means, electronic or mechanical, including photocopy, recording, or any information storage and retrieval system, without permission in writing from the publisher.

Requests for permission to make copies of any part of the work should be mailed to: Permissions, Jove Publications, Inc., 200 Madison Avenue, New York, N.Y. 10016

Eight previous printings
First Jove edition published April 1979
New Jove edition published February 1981

10 9 8 7 6 5 4 3 2 1

Printed in the United States of America

Jove books are published by Jove Publications, Inc.
200 Madison Avenue, New York, N.Y. 10016

1

"I WILL not marry him, Mama!"

"Virginia Stuyvesant Clay, you will do as you are told!" came the sharp reply.

Mrs. Clay rose impatiently from her seat and walked across the large, over-ornate room to stare down at her daughter.

"Do you know what you are saying, girl?" she asked, and her voice was harsh. "You are refusing to marry an Englishman who in a very short time will be a Duke. A Duke! Do you hear? There are only twenty-six—or is it twenty-nine—of them, and you will be a Duchess. That will teach Mrs. Astor to give herself airs and treat me as if I were a nobody. The day I see you come down the aisle as a future Duchess, Virginia, I think I shall want to die I shall be so happy."

"But, Mama, he has never even seen me!" Virginia expostulated.

"What has that got to do with it?" Mrs. Clay inquired. "It may be 1902 and the beginning of a new century, but in Europe, and of course in the East, marriages are always arranged by the parents of the bride and groom, and a very sensible method it is and one which turns out extremely well for all the parties concerned."

"You know as well as I do that this man . . ."

"The Marquess of Camberford," Mrs. Clay interposed.

"The Marquess then," Virginia went on, "is marrying me for my money. He is not interested in anything else."

"Now, Virginia, that is a ridiculous way to talk," her mother replied. "The Duchess is an old friend of mine, in fact, a very old friend. It must be nearly ten years since your papa and I met her when we were travelling in Europe, and most graciously she asked us to attend a Ball she was giving at their Castle."

"You had to pay for the tickets," Virginia interrupted.

"That is beside the point," Mrs. Clay answered loftily. "It was a Charity Ball and I have never pretended otherwise. But after it was over I communicated with the Duchess and helped her with various of her pet schemes—and very grateful to me she was."

"Grateful for the money," Virginia said quietly, but Mrs. Clay pretended not to have heard her.

"And so we kept up a correspondence," she continued. "I have regularly sent Her Grace presents at Christmas, for which she always thanked me most effusively, and when she wrote to me that she believed I had a daughter of marriageable age you will understand that I felt that all those thousands of dollars I have sent her from year to year have really begun to pay a dividend."

"But I have no desire to be a dividend, Mama, and though the Duchess may be charming, you have never seen her son."

"I have seen pictures of him, though," Mrs. Clay replied, "and very handsome he is, to be sure. He is not a beardless boy by any means. Twenty-eight last year. A man, Virginia! A man who will look after you and take care of all that ridiculous fortune your father left you and which should have been entirely in my control until you were married."

"Oh, Mama, must we go into this again? You are rich, terribly rich, and the fact that Papa left us his fortune in equal parts is surely of no consequence. As far as I am concerned you can have everything I possess—and then see if this Marquess would be so interested in me!"

"Virginia, I think you are the most ungrateful girl alive!" Mrs. Clay cried. "Here you have the opportunity of which every girl dreams. You will be marrying one of the most important men in England, indeed in the world. Can you imagine what your friends will say? Think of Millie and that Windrop girl, whatever her name is. And Nancy Duep and Gloriana. They will be green with envy, that is what they will be! Why, you will be asked to Buckingham Palace and you will go to dinner with the new King and Queen with a crown on your head."

"A tiara," Virginia corrected.

"Well, a tiara then, and I shall see to it that at your wedding you have the finest and biggest one of any woman in England. Do you realise what your marriage is going to look like in the newspapers?"

"I am not going to marry anyone I have not seen," Virginia said firmly.

"You will do as you're told," her mother replied angrily. "They have always said that Mrs. Rosenburg threatened her daughter with a horse-whip because she refused to marry the Duke of Melchester. Well, whatever threat she used it was pretty effective, and though Pauline may have been one of the first American Duchesses in London

Society there is plenty of room for another, and that is going to be you!"

"But I have no wish to be a Duchess, Mama. Why can you not understand? Besides, things have changed."

"In that way?" Mrs. Clay asked sharply. "Only in the fact that we have more Englishmen coming to America and more rich American families travelling in Europe than ever before. Why, your uncle was saying only the other day that they are thinking of building new Atlantic liners to carry people from this country abroad and that 1907 might well be a boom year in shipbuilding."

"So if we invest our money in that," Virginia said, "we shall make more dollars than we have already. What for?"

"What for?" Mrs. Clay repeated, and then made a gesture of impatience. "Will you stop talking about money in that derogatory way, Virginia, you are always doing it. You ought to be grateful that you have so much."

"I am not grateful if it means I have got to marry a man I have never met, whom I have never seen, and whose only interest in me is the dollars I will bring him."

"Now, Virginia, it is not like that at all," Mrs. Clay objected almost peevishly. "As I have told you, the Duchess and I have always been friends and she has written to me to suggest that a marriage of her son to my daughter would be a charming climax to our long friendship. What could be more delightful or, indeed, more practical than that idea?"

"How much has she asked you to pay for the privilege of marrying into the English aristocracy?" Virginia inquired.

"I am not going to answer that question! I think it is the type of remark which sounds extremely vulgar on a young girl's lips. You can leave all matters of business to me and to your uncle."

"I have asked you how much," Virginia insisted. Her voice was quiet and yet determined.

"And I am not going to tell you," Mrs. Clay snapped.

"Then it is what I suspected," Virginia said. "The Duchess wants a certain sum down. She is not content with my fortune which her son will control and has asked for more. I heard Uncle saying something to that effect, but you both shut up when I came into the room. How much is it?"

"I have told you it is none of your business," Mrs. Clay replied.

"But it is my business," Virginia protested. "I am the sacrifice, am I not, on this altar of snobbery?"

"Sarcastic remarks like that are not going to ingratiate you with English Society," Mrs. Clay warned her. "I cannot think why I could not have had a nice, quiet, obedient daughter like that Belmont girl who comes here sometimes."

"She comes here because you ask her," Virginia retorted. "She is no friend of mine. If ever a girl was half-witted it is Bella Belmont."

"Nevertheless, she is pretty, sweetly spoken and easy to manage," Mrs. Clay replied. "That is all I have ever asked for in a daughter."

"And I am what you have got."

"Yes, you are what I have got," Mrs. Clay repeated, "and so, Virginia, you will marry the Marquess of Camberford if I have to drag you screaming to the altar. Let us stop arguing about it and start planning your trousseau. There is very little time. He will be here in three weeks."

"Then let us wait until he arrives, Mama, before I give you my answer."

"That is not quite the point," Mrs. Clay replied a little uncomfortably.

She walked across the room, her silk petticoats rustling beneath her gown of green satin trimmed with pleated chiffon frills.

"What do you mean?" Virginia inquired.

"The Marquess is in a hurry," Mrs. Clay answered. "He arrives on April the twenty-ninth and you are to be married the following day."

For a moment there was a stupefied silence, and then a cry of utter incredulity.

"Married the following day! Are you mad, Mama? I would no more marry this fortune-hunter on April the thirtieth than fly over the moon! How dare he suggest such a thing? And how dare you even contemplate it?"

For a moment Mrs. Clay seemed nonplussed. Turning round to face her daughter she saw the girl put her hand up to her forehead and give a little groan as she sank back in the chair.

"What is the matter, Virginia? Is it one of your heads?"

"I feel terrible," Virginia replied. "I do not know what it is, Mama, but the medicine that last doctor gave me has made me feel worse than ever."

"He thinks you are anaemic," Mrs. Clay said, "and he wants you to build up your strength. Did you have your glass of wine at eleven o'clock?"

"I tried to drink it," Virginia replied, "but I really could not manage a whole glass."

"Now, Virginia, you know the doctor said that red wine makes good red blood. What about a glass of sherry before luncheon?"

"No, no, I want nothing," Virginia protested. "And I certainly do not feel like eating a big meal with this headache."

"You must eat sensibly," Mrs. Clay said sharply. "I know Chef has been making those special éclairs that you like so much; and I told him to see that you had an angel cake for tea."

"I do not want it, Mama, it makes me feel sick!" Virginia cried.

"We have got to do something to get the roses into your cheeks before the Marquess arrives."

Virginia gave a deep sigh.

"Listen, Mama, we cannot go on arguing like this for three weeks until he arrives. I am not going to marry this Englishman, Duke or no Duke, and nothing will persuade me to do so!"

There was a tense silence. Then Mrs. Clay said:

"Very well, Virginia, if you feel like that, I have made other arrangements."

"You have?" Virginia asked with a sudden relief in her voice. "Oh, Mama, why did you torture me? You know I have no desire to be married. What other arrangements have you made?"

"I have decided," Mrs. Clay said slowly, "that if you will not do as I wish, if you are not prepared to behave as any normal girl would do in the circumstances, then you are no longer a daughter of mine! I shall send you to your Aunt Louise."

"Aunt Louise!" Virginia echoed in an incredulous tone. "But . . . Aunt Louise is a nun! She runs a House of Correction."

"Exactly!" Mrs. Clay said. "And that is where you will live, Virginia, until you are twenty-five. For although you may have money of your own, you will remember that your father made me your Guardian."

"But, Mama, you cannot really mean that you would send me away?"

"I do mean it, Virginia. You may be my only child and I may have spoilt you the whole of your life, but you are not going to ruin every dream I have ever had of being the queen of New York Society. You can make a brilliant marriage or go to your aunt. Take your choice. That is my last word!"

"But you cannot mean it, it is impossible," Virginia whispered.

"I do mean it. You may think that, because I have always spoilt you, I will not keep my word. But you have always known that if I determine to get my own way I get it," Mrs. Clay asserted. "I did not push your father into being a multimillionaire without learning that if a person's will is strong enough he can get everything in the world that he wants. This is an ultimatum, Virginia! I warn you that I shall not waver in carrying out my threat."

There was silence. Virginia's hands were up to her face.

"Well, have I your answer?" Mrs. Clay asked, and her harsh voice seemed to echo around the room.

Virginia took her hands from her face and stared up at her mother.

"I cannot . . . believe it!" she faltered. "I cannot believe that . . . you . . . my mother . . . would . . . treat me like this."

"You will thank me for it when you are older," Mrs. Clay replied. "Now, Virginia, have I your promise that you will marry the Marquess the day after he arrives, and that you will go back to Europe with him as his wife?"

Virginia rose from the chair and walked toward her mother.

"I cannot promise you, Mama! How can I tie myself to a man I have never seen, who wants me only for my money? I do want to be married one day, but I want to marry someone I love and who loves me."

Mrs. Clay threw back her head and laughed. It was an ugly sound with no humour in it.

"Someone who loves you!" she repeated mockingly. "Do you really believe that is possible? Are you really so stupid, so thick in the head, that you imagine any man would love you for yourself? Come here!"

She caught hold of her daughter's arm and dragged her in front of a large, gilt mirror which hung on a wall of the drawing-room between two windows.

"Look at yourself! Take a good look!" Mrs. Clay said

cruelly. "And then find me the man who would marry you for anything but your fortune. Look! Look at yourself for what you are!"

Almost as if she were mesmerised into doing what her mother commanded, Virginia stared into the mirror. She saw her mother, thin almost to the point of boniness, with a small, elegant waist accentuated by her expensive gown and the jewels glittering round her long neck: a handsome woman and one who would stand out even in a room crowded with her own elegant contemporaries.

Then she looked at herself: small—hardly up to her mother's shoulder—and bulging with fat until she appeared utterly grotesque. Her eyes were lost in rolls of pink fat which puffed out her cheeks and gave her a number of double chins which almost hid her neck. Her balloon-like arms showed through the thin net of her sleeves; her hands, which went almost instinctively towards her face, were red and podgy.

She barely had a waist and in circumference she was three times the size of her mother. Her dress looked hideous, but she knew it would not have seemed so repulsive on anyone of a normal size. Her hair was lank and lifeless and of an indecisive colour which made its fashionable coiffure seem a mockery.

She stared and stared at herself and then heard her mother say almost in a tone of disgust:

"Now do you understand what I am talking about?"

Virginia covered her eyes with her fat fingers.

"I . . . know," she said, and her voice broke. "I look . . . terrible. The doctors . . . promise that . . . that I shall get . . . thinner. It is just that . . . I feel . . . so . . . ill."

"Promises! Promises!" Mrs. Clay exclaimed. "They have all said they will slim you down, they will make you feel better, that it is only a question of time. I wonder how many thousand dollars I have spent on doctors in the last five years? It is hoped that when you are married you will get thinner! Who knows, a miracle might happen!"

Virginia turned from the mirror.

"Perhaps when he sees me he will refuse to marry me," she said, and there was almost a tone of hope in her voice.

"That is one thing he will not do," Mrs. Clay said confidently.

"Why not?" Virginia asked.

"Because, my dear, you will be tied up with gilt ribbons

and I am sharp enough to realise that the Marquess is desperately in need of that money or the Duchess would not have written to me."

"How much are you giving him?" Virginia demanded.

"Do you really want to know?" Mrs. Clay inquired. "Would you not prefer to go on believing in love's young dream? Hoping that Prince Charming will pop down the chimney and fall in love with you at first sight? No, my girl, you had better know the truth! Whatever you look like, you have no need to crawl on your knees to the English aristocracy. They are getting their pound of flesh and the truth should give you a bit of confidence in yourself."

"Well, what is the truth?" Virginia asked. "How much are you giving him?"

"Two million dollars!" Mrs. Clay said, enunciating the words very slowly. "And if you translate that into English currency you will find it is four hundred thousand pounds—quite a valuable gift for any bridegroom to receive with his blushing bride."

Virginia gave a little moan and sat down on the sofa.

"And now," Mrs. Clay said briskly, "let us have no more hysterics. You will be married, Virginia, on April the thirtieth. If you refuse, you will be sent to your Aunt Louise and I shall announce to the world that my daughter has gone into a convent for the next seven years. Before you are free to leave you will find plenty of time to reflect on whether the advantages of being an English Duchess might not have exceeded the misery and discomfort of your aunt's House of Correction."

There was no answer from the sofa and Virginia turned to hide her face in one of the silk cushions. Twisted, her body looked gross and almost malformed. For a moment Mrs. Clay stood looking at her; then her lips tightened and her prominent chin looked firmer and more determined than ever.

"My God! What did I do to deserve that?" she asked, but her voice was so low it was doubtful if Virginia heard her.

In the days that followed Virginia seemed hardly conscious of what was happening. It was almost as if the shock of her mother's revelation, and the decision she had been forced to make against her will, had sapped her last ounce of strength.

The doctor came daily and her diet was altered almost

every twenty-four hours. Nourishing dishes of every sort and description were forced upon her. Rare delicacies from all over America were procured by employees of the Clay Corporation which spread the whole length and breadth of the continent.

Virginia was forced to drink ox blood for her anaemia. Cream from Jersey cows was brought to New York from the Clay ranch so that it should be pure and uncontaminated by city air. Vegetables and fruit from the Clay estates in Virginia, after which she had been christened, were carried by train hundreds of miles to tempt her appetite and force a reluctant colour into her flabby cheeks. Champagne from France; sherry from Spain; caviar from Russia; *pâté de foie gras* from Strasbourg, were only some of the delicacies which she ate simply and solely because there was such a fuss if she made no attempt to do so.

She felt sometimes as if she moved in a dream and that everything she did and said was unreal. She stood for hours having her *trousseau* fitted and was hardly aware that she was more tired at the end of the ordeal than she had been at the beginning.

Only when she was alone in her bedroom did she ask herself if there was any method of escape. Sometimes she would pretend to herself that she could creep from her room, run down the great marble staircase, unbar the heavy, mahogany door and find herself free and unfettered on Fifth Avenue. But she knew, even while she pretended, that it was impossible. She felt too tired, too ill, even to drag herself out of bed in the morning, let alone to run away.

Sometimes it seemed to her as if someone who was not herself was inside her brain and laughing at her. She could almost hear this other person's laughter. "You are fat and useless!" "Fat and stupid!" "Fat and ugly!" "Fat and spineless!" The voice would taunt her, and sometimes it would say over and over again: "He is marrying you for your money! He is marrying you for your money! He is marrying you for your money!"

When the voice was speaking she seemed to see her money, great piles of it, golden and glittering, filling up her room, reaching the ceiling, and then tipping over, sliding towards her, enveloping her with its hard, cold glitter.

"Really, Virginia," her mother said to her once, "you behave as if you were drugged. I must speak to Dr.

Hausell—or was that the last one? I really cannot keep count of their names—and tell him that I will not tolerate your taking narcotics."

But Virginia knew it was not the doctor's medicines, half of which she poured away without bothering to take them. It was something in herself that was trying to escape from reality, something that was running away almost as effectively as if she really did step through the front door into the busy traffic outside.

"The Marquess arrives tomorrow," she heard her mother say, and felt nothing, not even a start of surprise.

She had long ago given up wondering what he looked like or what would be her reaction to him. She just felt numb and miserable. But that night the mocking voice was there. "He is marrying you for your money! He is marrying you for your money!" And all her bedroom was filled with gold. The bed was gold and the sheets were stiff so that she could not bend them. She felt as if her hands were weighed down with it.

Gold! Gold! Gold! She thought that even what she ate tasted like gold and the champagne they kept forcing on her had flecks of real gold bubbling in it.

Mrs. Clay had arranged an enormous reception for the night of the Marquess's arrival. At the back of the Clay house a marquee had been erected and for days workmen had been putting down a special floor, carrying in banks of exotic flowers, bringing the Clay treasures from the bank to ornament the walls.

Mrs. Clay was in her element.

"The marriage shall be in the drawing-room," she had decided. "The whole room will be a bower of white orchids. But for the reception the motif shall be gay. Pink, I think, shall be the predominant colour and Virginia shall wear pink—pink tulle decorated with rosebuds and a wreath of rosebuds in her hair."

People talked afterwards of the Clay reception given for the Marquess as one of the highlights of New York entertaining. But unfortunately the Marquess himself was not there. Owing to unexpectedly rough seas in the Atlantic, his ship did not dock until four o'clock in the morning and by the time he reached the hotel where he was staying the reception was over.

Virginia, who was sent to bed about one o'clock, so that she should be fresh for the ceremony the following day, had a sneaking feeling that her mother was secretly relieved that the Marquess had not seen her. Ill and tired though she was, she was astute enough to realise that, now that the moment of meeting was actually upon them, Mrs. Clay was a little apprehensive as to what the Marquess would think of his bride.

Virginia wondered what lies her mother had told in writing to the Duchess. How had she described her only daughter? She was quite certain that in her anxiety to obtain the Marquess as a son-in-law, her mother would certainly not have been truthful about the appearance of his future wife.

In her own room Virginia dragged the wreath of pink rosebuds from her limp hair and stared at herself in the mirror. It seemed to her that in the last three weeks she had grown not slimmer but even fatter. The sinus trouble from which she habitually suffered had swollen the flesh round her eyes so that they were almost indiscernible amongst mountains of flesh, and she noticed that the little cracks that had been forming for some time at the corners of her lips were more pronounced than ever. They were always bad in the winter, but usually by the spring they had gone. Her chilblains were itching, too, though the warm weather should have cured them.

She pulled off her dress and realised from the sense of relief she experienced that her waistband had been too tight. Hurriedly she got into her nightgown, and, deliberately avoiding the mirror, she crept between the sheets of her bed.

"Perhaps I should have gone to Aunt Louise," she said aloud, and then with a little sob she added: "I wish I were dead! Oh God! I wish I were dead!"

In the morning, however, she found herself alive and in the centre of a hive of activity. Her mother came into her room before she had been called, pulling back the curtains and ringing the bell, not once but a dozen times.

"I have already received a note from the Marquess," she said in tones of satisfaction. "I must say I do enjoy the good manners of the English aristocracy. He wrote it as soon as he arrived in New York, apologising that the ship was late—as if it were his fault, poor man—and saying how much he regretted the inconvenience I had experienced at the reception I had given in his honour. But I cannot help feeling things have worked out for the best. The first time you will see each other is when the Bishop joins you as man and wife."

Virginia said nothing and after a moment Mrs. Clay went on:

"It is a lovely day! The sun is shining and I rather regret now that I did not have you married at St. Thomas's. But the drawing-room looks beautiful and you had better start getting up, Virginia. You do not want to begin your married life by keeping your husband waiting. There is nothing that irritates a man more."

"I feel ill," Virginia groaned.

"That is nerves, dear, and well you know it. Drink up your milk and later, just before the ceremony, you shall have a glass of champagne."

"I do not want any champagne," Virginia protested. "It tastes acid and it gives me indigestion."

"Well, you will need something. What was it the doctor said you were to have?"

Virginia did not answer. She knew that whatever the doctor prescribed it would be countermanded by her mother, who had her own ideas about what stimulated or invigorated anyone who felt ill.

"Drink some coffee," Mrs. Clay commanded. "I am just sending for a pot. I am sure I cannot get through this morning without a dozen cups."

When the coffee arrived she poured out a large cup for Virginia and added several spoonfuls of sugar.

"Sugar for energy," she said brightly. "I always think coffee gives one a real lift!"

"It makes my heart race," Virginia said sulkily. "Honestly, Mama, I would much rather not drink coffee today."

"For goodness' sake, Virginia, must you argue about everything?" Mrs. Clay demanded. "Drink it up and do as you are told. I know what is best for you, as I always have. Now for your bath and the maids will get your clothes all ready on the bed. I am sure some last-minute touches will be necessary and I do not want a rush. You are to be ready and waiting before I go downstairs to receive the guests."

It was easier to obey than to argue. Virginia had a hot bath, and when she came out of it she felt so giddy that she had to sit for nearly five minutes on a chair in the bathroom before she could finish drying herself.

Then the hairdresser arrived. The veil was arranged on her head, held, as Virginia noted without surprise, by an enormous diamond tiara so large and set with such brilliant stones that she felt that even on anyone as tall as her mother it would have looked vulgar and overpowering. On herself it was a disaster.

"Now that is what I call a crown—I mean a tiara!" Mrs. Clay said, coming into the room and surveying her with satisfaction. "Do not ask me what it has cost because your papa, if he were alive, poor man, would have a stroke. He never believed that money should be locked up in jewellery. He liked to have it mobile at his finger-tips."

"It is very magnificent," Virginia said faintly.

"It is my wedding present to you, dear," Mrs. Clay said. "I thought you would be pleased. And what do you think? Mrs. Astor has accepted an invitation to be here at the wedding! I wondered why she had not replied, but she has been away. I thought she would not be able to resist coming to see what the Marquess is like. And I can tell you one thing, he is too good-looking to need a title."

"Have you seen him?" Virginia asked.

"Have I seen him!" Mrs. Clay repeated. "He was round here at half past nine, full of apologies about last night and being charming, yes, charming, about everything. Virginia, all I can say is that you are the luckiest girl who ever trod the soil of the United States of America. I could not help thinking as I was talking to him that if I were twenty-five years younger it would not be you, Virginia, who would be marrying him but me!"

Mrs. Clay laughed, but there was no answering smile on Virginia's lips.

"Have you given him the money?" she asked.

"Do not be so vulgar," Mrs. Clay admonished. "And if you want your marriage to be a success never mention the money to your husband under any circumstances. If I had any sense I would not have told you about it. But there, I never was good at keeping a secret and my tongue runs away with me. Promise me, Virginia, you will behave like a lady and leave all matters of finance to your husband."

"I have no choice in the matter," Virginia replied. "As you well know, Papa left the custody of my money to you, and, if I married, to my husband until I am twenty-five. I dare say the noble Marquess, if I beg him to do so, will give me a little pin-money!"

"Virginia, I will not tolerate your talking in that rude, sarcastic manner!" Mrs. Clay's voice rose angrily. "The Marquess is one of the most delightful, and certainly one of the most handsome, young men I have ever seen. All New York will be crazy about him. You will be the envy of every girl in the whole city. Now, behave yourself, and remember there are two sides to the bargain. He, too, might have wanted to fall in love!"

Mrs. Clay went from the room and slammed the door. Virginia put her head in her hands. As always in an argument with her mother, she was the loser. From years of arguing with her husband, Mrs. Clay had the knack of invariably having the last word, of always leaving those who argued with her wounded.

The coffee that her mother had forced her to drink seemed to have made her heart beat more violently than usual. It had also brought a flush to her cheeks and she felt suddenly that the room was airless, that she was unable to breathe.

She asked the maid to open the window. The weather outside was soft and mild. As she was assisted into her wedding-dress she wondered if she would have the strength to walk up the long, crowded drawing-room on her uncle's arm.

At last she was ready. The dress, with its tier upon tier of white Brussels lace, would have been lovely, Virginia thought, if it had not been so monstrously big. The veil flowed down her back from the huge, glittering tiara, and she felt, for a moment, that she looked like an outsize fairy on the Christmas tree.

She gave a bitter laugh. As she did so, there was a knock at the door and a footman entered bearing a glass of champagne on a silver salver.

"Your mother's compliments, Miss Virginia, and you are to drink every drop."

Virginia took it and had a sip, feeling that perhaps it might, indeed, make her breathing easier. The black footman, whom she hardly recognised in a new, very ornate uniform, powdered wig and clean white cotton gloves, smiled.

"I sure wishes you luck, Miss Virginia."

"Thank you," Virginia said mechanically.

She set the empty glass down on her dressing-table and heard her uncle's voice call her from the doorway.

"Are you ready, Virginia? They are waiting for you."

"I am ready, Uncle."

She moved towards him, saw the expression of admiration on his face, and, at the same time, realised it was for the tiara and not herself.

"Wait a minute, miss," one of the maids said. "You

haven't got the veil over your face. There's a bit of tulle for you to wear until you are married and then you can pull it aside and not upset the veil at the back."

"Thank you," Virginia murmured.

The maid fitted the tulle veil over her face. It seemed to block out the last vestige of air in the room and her heart appeared to be thumping more violently than ever.

"It is nerves," she thought to herself. She put her hand, in its white kid glove, on her uncle's arm and picked up her bouquet of tuberoses and lilies of the valley. They started to walk slowly downstairs to the drawing-room.

Faint music could barely be heard, drowned by the chatter of hundreds of voices. Those who had not managed to find a seat amongst the white orchids were crowded out on to the stairway. As they stood aside to let Virginia and her uncle pass, murmuring expressions of goodwill, she bent her head and made no attempt to answer them. Every step was an effort and she was thankful for the support of her uncle's arm.

Moving up the room, Virginia felt almost as if her uncle was towing her along, that if he were not there she would move backwards instead of forwards. She raised her eyes and had a quick glimpse of the Bishop. On one side of him stood her mother with an expression of delight and triumph on her face; on the other stood a man.

She had not expected the Marquess to be so tall, so broad-shouldered, nor, indeed, so dark. She had always imagined that Englishmen were fair, but he was dark and, indeed, her mother had been right. He was the most handsome man she had ever seen in her life.

She must have tightened her grip on her uncle's arm, because he looked down at her and she heard him ask:

"Are you all right, Virginia?"

They had reached the end of the drawing-room and now she was standing in front of the Bishop with the Marquess beside her. She knew without looking up that he turned his head to look at her and she was thankful for her veil; thankful, too, that because he was so tall he would see little but the brilliant, glittering tiara on her bent head.

The service began.

"Wilt thou take this man to be thy wedded husband . . . for better, for worse, for richer, for poorer . . . in sickness and in health . . . ?"

She heard her own voice, faint and seeming to come from a long distance, respond:

"I will."

She heard his responses, firm, strong and somehow completely impersonal. His voice was strange—an English voice—and she wondered if they would ever be able to communicate with each other, she and this stranger to whom she was giving herself in marriage.

The ceremony was over. Someone was taking the veil from her face; her husband was leading her down the stairs to the great marquee which had been transformed into a reception room with a gigantic five-tier cake in the centre of it.

She picked her way warily, feeling somehow as if her feet might trip over her dress. She could not bear to look at the Marquess, although she held his arm. She was conscious of his nearness; conscious, too, that he was tense.

Her mother was chattering beside them.

"This way, Marquess . . . Oh, no, I must not call you that now, must I? Sebastian! What a delightful name! Sebastian and Virginia go so well together, do they not? I hope that you enjoyed the service. The Bishop of New York is such a delightful man—a very old friend. I would have had no one but him marry you and dear Virginia."

They had reached the table on which rested the huge cake. It stood towering above them.

"A glass of champagne!" Mrs. Clay was saying. "Then, of course, you will receive the guests; after that you must cut the cake. I shall stand here. They will file past you. All our friends are so anxious to meet you, Marquess . . . I mean, Sebastian. You are a very important visitor to New York today. Now I must drink your health before anyone else."

"Champagne! Champagne!" Mrs. Clay was speaking to one of the footmen. "A glass for you, Sebastian! A glass for Virginia. To you both, my dears! May you be happy ever after."

"Thank you, Mrs. Clay, that is very kind of you!" His voice was deep, quiet and controlled.

"And now you and Virginia must drink to each other," Mrs. Clay insisted.

The Marquess turned towards her and Virginia was compelled to raise her eyes. She looked up at him; looked into a strange, incredibly handsome face and saw in his eyes not the disgust she had expected but a look of almost cynical indifference that was quite unmistakable. She stared at him, startled because it was not at all what she had anticipated.

"Your good health, Virginia!" she heard him say. Then, as she strove to respond, she found that the room was spinning round her; the wedding cake was tilting over. And she knew it was not a cake but money—golden, glittering money! It was falling, tumbling, beating down upon her, and she could no longer resist it.

She felt herself begin to crumple beneath the weight of it and knew, as she heard someone's scream—she thought it was her mother and yet she was not certain—that the gold enveloped her and there was no escape!

2

THERE was the sound of birds singing. Virginia found herself listening to them, trying to distinguish one from the other. Once, long ago, she would have known each songbird by name.

Very slowly, with an effort, she opened her eyes. A cloud of red, white and yellow butterflies was moving against a vivid blue sky, and she had a feeling of enchantment and of happiness. Suddenly a face appeared between her and the sky and a voice, very softly and yet with a note of excitement in it, said:

"You are awake! Virginia, you are awake!"

Virginia tried to speak and thought for a moment that her throat was paralysed. Then hardly above a whisper she asked:

"Who . . . are you?"

"I am your aunt, Virginia—Aunt Ella May! Do you remember me?"

"I . . . remember . . . you." The words were hardly audible. Virginia's eyes closed and she fell asleep.

Hours later, or maybe it was days, she came back to consciousness. The birds were now silent, but when she opened her eyes the butterflies were still there and she realised that it must be the heat of the day. She could see the wistaria blossom trailing over the edge of what she knew must be the verandah on which she was lying. A strong arm lifted her and a glass was held to her lips.

"Drink, Virginia, it will do you good," her aunt's voice said.

She drank obediently. It was delicious, but when she had had a few sips the glass was taken away.

"Where . . . am . . . I?" Virginia asked, her eyes on the butterflies. They seemed to symbolise to her something she was trying to capture, or was it something she had lost?

"You are in my house," her aunt replied. "I am looking after you."

"Aunt . . . Ella . . . May," Virginia stammered. "I . . . remember . . . now; you are . . . a nurse. Have I . . . been ill?"

"Yes, dear, very ill."

"What was . . . wrong . . . with me?"

"I do not think you want to talk about it now," her aunt replied. "Lie still. In a little while I will give you another drink."

"I want it . . now," Virginia insisted. "I am . . . thirsty."

A glass was lifted to her lips and she tried to recognise what was in the delicious liquid which seemed to relieve the dryness of her throat.

"H . . . Honey!" she said aloud when she had finished drinking.

Her aunt smiled.

"And watercress and celery and other green vegetables."

"Vegetables?" Virginia was surprised, but it was too much of an effort to pursue the subject. "How long . . . have I . . . been here?"

"A long time," her aunt replied.

Virginia was silent. Then she said:

"I am trying . . . to remember. I fell . . . Was there an . . . accident?"

"Do not worry about it now," her aunt begged. "Just be content to sleep."

"I feel as if I have . . . slept for a . . . very long . . . time," Virginia murmured, and was already asleep before she had said the last word.

When she woke again, this time it was evening. She was inside the house. The curtains were pulled—gay, chintz curtains, not expensive but pretty. The room was small with a low ceiling, and though it was summer there was a fire burning in the grate.

Virginia stirred and her aunt rose from the fireplace and came towards her.

"You are awake again," she said. "Do you think you could swallow a little soup?"

Virginia nodded. Her aunt fed her. The soup was even more delicious than the honey drink had been. When she had finished quite an amount of it Virginia felt less tired.

"I am . . . glad to . . . see you, Aunt . . . Ella . . . May," she said, choosing her words carefully as if it was hard to remember them. "I often thought of you . . . but you never came . . . to call on us . . . in New York."

"No, dear," her aunt replied gently.

Memory came back to Virginia—of raised voices—of her father, furiously angry as he had been so often when people crossed him—of her mother, angry too—of the slamming of doors and Aunt Ella May leaving the house, with tears in her eyes but looking determined, unconquered.

"I . . . remember," Virginia said aloud. "You went . . . away."

"Yes, dear," Aunt Ella May answered. "I went away to be married. But I came to your wedding because your mother asked me to do so."

"My . . . wedding!" Virginia was very still. Then she said as if to herself: "The cake . . . fell on me and . . . and the gold! My head . . . hurt. It must have been that big . . . ugly . . . tiara."

"When you fell down," Aunt Ella May said, "the tiara rolled over and over on the floor."

Virginia felt her lips twitch, then she gave a weak, shaky laugh.

"I always did think tiaras were ridiculously useless!" Aunt Ella May smiled.

"Mama . . . called it a . . . crown," Virginia said, and they laughed together.

Suddenly the laughter died.

"Mama!" Virginia exclaimed in a frightened voice. "She will be . . . angry with me for being . . . ill. Why did she . . . let me come to . . . you?"

Her aunt rose from the bedside.

"We will talk about it another time, dear."

"No, now," Virginia said insistently. "I want . . . to know. She is . . . angry, is she not?"

"I do not want to upset you," Aunt Ella May said in her soft voice. "But your mother is not angry, Virginia dear. You see, she is dead!"

Virginia stared up at her in surprise.

"Dead!" she said slowly. "I somehow never thought . . .

that Mama would . . . die. She always . . . seemed so strong, so . . . so indestructible. Is . . . is that why I am with . . . you?"

"Yes, dear."

Afterwards it seemed to Virginia that it took days of questioning, of broken sentences, of answers which seemed not to frighten or upset her but merely to make her sleepy, before she discovered what had happened. But, actually, Aunt Ella May told her later that she was so curious that she found out the truth within twenty-four hours of regaining consciousness.

"After your collapse," her aunt related, "your mother worked herself into a tremendous state of anger and frustration. She thought you were pretending to be ill to avoid meeting the guests, and that you had fallen through clumsiness. She was incensed to see your tiara lying on the floor, and even more incensed to find how difficult it was to lift you to your feet."

"Go on!" Virginia whispered.

"Your dress and your tulle veil got in the way, but finally, when they picked you up and carried you into an anteroom off the drawing-room, where all the guests were congregated, your mother screamed furiously that the wedding must go on. 'Virginia will join us as soon as she has recovered! Someone can stay with her; I do not care who it is.' It was then that I spoke. 'I will look after her,' I said.

" 'Oh, it is you, Ella May, is it?' your mother said to me. 'Well, you ought to be good at nursing, you have had enough practice. Get that child on her feet as quickly as possible!' And she went out of the room and shut the door.

"But when I looked at you I realised all too clearly that it was not going to be possible to get you on your feet for a very long time.

"The doctors, when they came to see you, had a lot of high-sounding names for it," Aunt Ella May continued, "but I will put it more simply to you. For years you had been stuffed like a Strasbourg goose with every sort of food that was poison to your system. Sugar, rich creamy milk, *pâtés* and delicacies, combined with the wine the doctors ordered, had converted what was naturally a strong young body into a monstrous mountain of unhealthy flesh. Not only could your heart not stand the strain, but the poisons rose into your brain and combined with the worry and unhappiness over your proposed marriage to give you what we country folk call brain-fever."

Virginia gave a little start.

"Brain-fever!" she cried. "Does that mean that I was mad?"

"Delirious," her aunt told her. "You talked about money most of the time. It was a word of which I have never been very fond and now I abominate it."

"I thought gold was pouring over me as I fell," Virginia said. "I can remember it quite clearly. The cake was toppling down too."

"That huge edifice of white, indigestible sugar!" her aunt exclaimed with a smile. "It was the best thing that could have happened to it."

"So I never went back to the wedding!" Virginia said. "Mama must have been furious."

"She was so angry," Aunt Ella May said, "that during the night she had a stroke."

"Oh, no!" Virginia cried. "Poor Mama! I must have been a terrible disappointment to her."

"I am afraid you were," her aunt agreed.

"She never loved me," Virginia said. "And although she talked about spoiling me, it only meant that she gave me presents when I did what she wanted. I was never allowed to do anything I wanted to do. I am afraid I shall shock you, Aunt Ella May, but I cannot be sorry that Mama is dead. She always made me feel as if I was drowning under a tidal wave and had no possible hope of saving myself."

"We will speak no ill of the dead," Aunt Ella May said briskly. "But I think even your mother's best friend would admit she was a difficult woman. She drove your father into being a multi-millionaire and he collapsed under the strain of it. She drove you, too, did she not?"

Virginia looked down.

"What happened," she asked, her voice hardly above a whisper, "to . . . him?"

"To your husband?" her aunt asked in a matter-of-fact tone. "He was the only person who seemed to keep his head after your mother's collapse. You were ill in one room and your mother in another and everyone was tearing about, making wild suggestions and getting nothing done! Lawyers, executors, all appeared like magic and cluttered up the place, so that it was almost impossible to get anything organised. It was then that I talked to your husband and suggested I take you away to my home in the country. I told him who I was; I told him of my qualifications, and he agreed instantly."

"So that is how I came to be here. Was . . . he angry too?" Virginia asked.

Her aunt shook her head.

"No, he was just sorry. As a matter of fact, Virginia, I liked him."

"I hated him!" Virginia declared. "And I still hate him! Now that Mama is dead I need no longer go on being married to him, need I?"

"We will talk about that another time," her aunt suggested.

"No I want to talk about it now," Virginia insisted. "You see, Aunt Ella May, Mama forced me to marry a man I had never seen before, simply because she wanted to show the other hostesses in New York that she could outdo them. She wanted to rival Mrs. Astor and there was nothing I could say or do which would alter her decision."

"Surely you could have refused?" her aunt said.

"I did," Virginia replied, "and Mama threatened that if I did she would sent me to Aunt Louise until I was twenty-five."

"To your Aunt Louise?" Aunt Ella May rose and walked across the room. "That was a wicked, wicked thing to do."

"So I had no choice." Virginia continued. "I had to do what she wished. But I hated that man. I never, never want to see him again!"

For the first time there was something like a note of passion in her quiet voice. Her aunt came back to her and lowered her gently back on the pillow.

"You are not to talk about it or think about it," she said. "There will be time for all this later on. You have been very ill, Virginia, and you have got to be a very sensible girl and build yourself up again. Do not worry about anything. It will all come right, I promise you."

For a moment Virginia lay tense, and then she said suddenly with a little chuckle:

"He must have hated me too. He did not know what he was getting until we stood together in front of the Bishop. I should think my face under that tiara must have given him quite a shock."

Her aunt sat down on the bed.

"Virginia," she said, "I love you. When you were a small child you always had a sense of humour. It was something both your father and your mother lacked. Anyone who can laugh at himself is my favourite person."

"I am not such a grump that I did not realise I looked a monstrosity," Virginia said. "Mama made me drink coffee and champagne all the morning, so that my face was hot and red and I just could not breathe under the veil. Oh, Aunt Ella May! Why was I born so hideous? Mama was good-looking when she was a girl—some people said she was lovely. And Papa was a handsome man, was he not?"

"They were a good-looking couple," Aunt Ella May agreed. "I wonder, Virginia, if you are strong enough for another shock?"

"What has happened now?" Virginia asked a little apprehensively.

"Wait a minute," her aunt said. "I want to sit you up." She propped her up against the pillows, and then she said: "Shut your eyes. This is a surprise, but a very nice one."

"You are sure?" Virginia asked with a sudden fear. "I have not got to see anybody, have I?"

"Just shut your eyes and trust me."

Virginia did as she was told. She heard her aunt walk across the room and then come back to the bedside.

"Now open your eyes," Aunt Ella May commanded.

Virginia, raising her eyelids, found herself staring into the face of a stranger. It took her the flash of a second to realise that her aunt was holding across the bed a large mirror. Then she thought she must be dreaming or, indeed, mad, for looking at her from the mirror was someone she had never seen before.

It was certainly a girl of about her age, a girl with very large eyes in a thin, pointed face. The cheek-bones were accentuated, the jaw-line sharp against the long neck, and hanging over the girl's shoulders was a great profusion of dead-white hair!

For a long time Virginia could only stare, and then in a voice that she hardly recognised as her own she asked:

"Is . . . that really . . . me?"

"That has always been you," her aunt smiled. "But the poor thing was hidden by the fat which distorted what should have been young, pretty, lithe and light into something grotesque and hideous."

Virginia put her hands up to her face.

"Look at my fingers," she said, "and my arms. Oh, Aunt Ella May! I would never recognise myself. And what has happened to my hair?"

"Brain-fever often makes a victim's hair go white," her aunt said. "But the colour will come back in time, when you get well and strong again. You see, Virginia, you are, after all, a very pretty girl."

"Pretty! How can I be pretty?" Virginia asked, but she saw an incredulous delight dawning in the eyes of the girl in the mirror—eyes that were dark grey with somehow a tinge of purple in them; eyes that were fringed with very long, dark lashes. And the moulding of the face, the straight little nose, and the arched eyebrows and smooth forehead were undoubtedly attributes of beauty.

"I do not . . . believe it," Virginia said, and suddenly, for the first time since she had come back to consciousness, she began to cry.

Her aunt put the mirror away and coming back to the bed lowered her down on to the pillows.

"I . . . cannot . . . b . . . believe it," Virginia whispered through her tears. "I cannot . . . believe it."

"It is true," her aunt said. "And now, Virginia, go to sleep. If you get too excited I shall be sorry I showed you yourself."

"It seems such a waste of time to go to sleep," Virginia complained. "I have got so much to think about." But she slept nevertheless.

Two weeks later she walked in from the garden and sat down on the verandah where her aunt was shelling peas for luncheon.

"I walked right to the wood and back," she boasted. "I am not in the least bit tired."

"Do not overdo it," Aunt Ella May warned her.

"I feel so light that it seems as if the wind might sweep me away up into the very tops of the trees," Virginia said.

"You are too light," her aunt said practically. "There is a chicken for lunch. If you do not eat a good portion of it, I shall send you back to bed."

"You would not be so cruel," Virginia protested. "Besides, there are such a lot of things I want to talk to you about. Do you realise, Aunt Ella May, that I have been so taken up with my looks that I have not had time to talk to you about my marriage?"

"I was going to discuss that with you," her aunt said.

"You see, I had a letter from your husband this morning."

"You had a letter from the Marquess?" Virginia asked.

"Yes," her aunt replied. "But he is now a Duke. You must realise, dear, that you are a Duchess!"

"It is the last thing I want to be," Virginia objected. "And somehow you have got to get rid of him."

"He has been very attentive," her aunt went on. "He writes every month to inquire about you."

"Why should he worry about me?" Virginia said. "He has got the money—the money Mama paid him to marry me—and all my own fortune if he wishes for it. I am not interested; he can have the lot."

"That is another thing I want to talk to you about," her aunt said. "With your mother's death, do you realise you are now one of the richest young women in all America?"

"It does not interest me," Virginia repeated. "I do not want anything more than I have got here."

Her aunt laughed.

"You would not be happy for long. You would find it very cramping."

"Do you find it so?" Virginia asked.

Her aunt smiled and shook her head.

"No, indeed, because it is my home. I came here when I married and at first we were very, very poor. Your father cut me out of the family life because I married the man I loved."

"Oh, Aunt Ella May! Is he alive?" Virginia asked.

"No, dear, he died two years ago. That was why I was glad, in a way, to be able to look after you. You see, I had been very lonely without my husband. We had no children and it was almost like having one, all those months when you lay there needing me, entirely dependent upon my ministrations."

"All those months!" Virginia said reflectively. "I never asked, Aunt Ella May, but how long have I been here?"

"One year and two months," her aunt replied.

Virginia looked aghast.

"All that time! And I did not recognise you?"

"No, dear, but you do now and that is all that matters. I can think of few things in my life that have given me more satisfaction than seeing you as you are today."

Virginia looked down at the unfashionable cotton dress that she wore, which was one of her aunt's taken in to fit her but, even so, still too large round the waist.

"It is a good thing you had something to lend me," she

said, and then added: "One thing I have decided, Aunt Ella May. I am going to stay here with you—that is, if you will have me. The only thing my money is good for is to pay my way."

"I will not take your money," her aunt said sharply. "None of it. I told your father when he cut me off that I would fend for myself and would never ask him for a cent. I have kept my promise; I am not going to break it now, not even for you."

"Do you mean to say that you have been paying for me all these months?" Virginia asked.

"You have not been very expensive," her aunt answered. "And if you have not had all the comforts you might have had in an expensive nursing-home, at least I have brought you back to life my way."

"The best way in the world," Virginia said loyally. "And do not worry, Aunt Ella May; if I ever went away I should stick to all the things you have taught me about fresh food and vegetables and how the only sugar one needs is the sweetness of honey from the bees in the garden."

"You are certainly the best advertisement I could have," her aunt said. "But, dear, the world outside is waiting for you and when you are a little stronger you have got to go back and face it."

"Why should I?" Virginia asked rebelliously.

"There is your husband, for one reason," her aunt replied, picking up a letter which lay beside her on the couch.

"I will not see him! I will never see him!" Virginia declared.

"Why? Are you afraid of him?" her aunt inquired.

"No, not afraid," Virginia explained, "but I despise him. He is a fortune-hunter, a man who would accept a bribe to marry a girl he had never seen."

"It sounds terrible, I agree," her aunt said. "At the same time, I must be honest with you, Virginia, and say that I like him. He was so calm and serious when all those people were screaming about the place. When your mother collapsed he carried her up to bed, sent for the doctor, organised the servants and, what was more, had everyone obeying him. I like a man like that. It reminded me of Clement, my husband, before he died."

"Well, I do not care whom he reminded you of," Virginia said a little rudely. "I mean to be rid of him."

"A divorce is not easily obtainable here," her aunt said quietly, "and it is far more difficult in England."

"But he cannot want to keep me!" Virginia exclaimed.

"That, of course, is for him to decide," her aunt replied. "His letters are always courteous. He is always inquiring if there is anything he can do. I suppose, Virginia, I ought to tell him that you are well again."

"No! No! You are not to do that! Do you hear, Aunt Ella May? You are not to! He might come to see me, and that I could not bear."

"There is no hurry," her aunt said quietly, "but he will have to know sooner or later."

"Why should he?"

"Because unless you stay boxed up here for the rest of your life people will know."

"What people? I have no friends."

"But there is always the press," her aunt said. "When you are feeling a little stronger, if you look in the bottom drawer of the bureau in the sitting-room you will find a lot of newspapers which I kept for you to see—photographs of your wedding—headlines about your illness. The bride of a Marquess was very much front-page news for days. Your mother's death of course accentuated the drama."

Virginia gave a little sob.

"Oh, Aunt Ella May! What am I to do?"

"I think you have to be grown-up about this," her aunt replied. "You see, Virginia, you have never really thought out things for yourself. Your mother did not let you and, although I know she was difficult, I think you were rather inclined to knuckle under her simply because you could not face up to rows. It is very un-American to be subservient. You have got to go forward into battle and defeat this bogey you have created for yourself of being afraid of people. After all, they are no different from you. Their hearts beat; they bleed if you prick them; and they, too, have feelings of apprehension and fear, of worry and oppression."

Virginia did not speak for a moment; then she asked:

"What do you want me to do?"

"That you must decide for yourself," her aunt answered.

"You mean I should ask him to come over here and see me?"

"I think very shortly we shall have to tell him that you have recovered. I think it might be rather amusing to see his face when he sees you as you are, remembering what you were like when he married you."

"I hate and despise him," Virginia protested. "The reason why I collapsed, Aunt Ella May, was that for three weeks after Mama had told me I had to marry him I lay awake at night saying, 'I hate you! I hate you!' Do you know, I even made a little image of a man out of a wax candle and I stuck little pins into it saying, 'Die! Die!' My nurse told me the Indians do that to someone they hate. But he didn't die. He arrived and I . . . married him."

Her voice broke for a moment on a little sob.

"You may want to laugh, remembering how ugly I was, but I used to dream that one day I would fall in love. I hoped I would find a man who would love me despite my looks and not for my money. I think at the back of my mind was the memory of how you stood up to Papa and insisted on marrying the man you loved. I was not very old at the time, but I remember hearing Mama and Papa saying what a fool you were and how only stupid people said that the world was well lost for love. But even then I knew you were right."

"Oh, you poor child!" Aunt Ella May said very quietly.

"I grew uglier and uglier," Virginia continued, "but that did not stop my dreaming. When I went to bed at night I used to tell myself a story. I was always the heroine and the hero fell in love with me because he did not know who I was.

"Sometimes I met him by chance in the park. Sometimes it was in a shop. I would lose Mama in a crowd or get separated from my attendants. And then, as I realised how terrible I looked, I used to pretend that he was blind. I went to read to him out of pity and he fell in love with my voice. Finally, we were married and were happy together because we loved each other for what we were inside, not for how we looked."

"Oh, Virginia dear! If only I had known," her aunt said. Then she added: "It would not have made any difference. I could not have come to you in that big, overpowering house and, anyway, your mother would not have let me."

"I think now, looking back, that my dreams became almost more real than my everyday life," Virginia said. "But do you know, Aunt Ella May, I tried to improve myself. I tried to be worthy of this man who wanted me and not my money. I worked very hard at my lessons when I did not get those terrible headaches. I used to get books out of the library which were very difficult to understand, but I forced myself to read them because I thought they would improve my brain."

"I am sure they did," Aunt Ella May said.

"I hope so," Virginia replied. "It was only when my headaches got so bad that it was difficult to concentrate, but I read an enormous amount. You will laugh, but I know all the history of America and of Great Britain and a great deal about France."

"I do not believe that knowledge is ever wasted," Aunt Ella May said.

"Now you understand," Virginia continued, "why the idea of being married to a man who wants me only for my money is like living in Hell. It betrays everything I believed in, all my dreams, all my ambitions, all the things that I have lived for these past five years since I started to grow up."

There was silence and then suddenly Virginia fell on her knees beside her aunt.

"Help me, Aunt Ella May!" she begged. "Help me be free of him! Now that I look like this—entirely owing to all you have done for me—now that I am a normal, ordinary girl, perhaps, just perhaps, I shall find the man of whom I have been dreaming. But first I must be free—free of this fortune-hunter. Please help me!"

Her aunt looked down at the small, eager face turned up to hers. "She is lovely," she thought. "It will not be hard to find not one man, but dozens, who will fall in love with her. But aways she will be suspicious of them. Always she will ask herself whether it is she or her money with which they are infatuated."

"Help me," Virginia pleaded and her big, violet-grey eyes with their long, dark lashes were desperate in their appeal.

Her aunt put down the bowl of shelled peas with a little bang.

"I will help you, Virginia," she said almost sharply, "but first let us prepare lunch. We shall need some good, nourishing food in us if we have got to tackle a problem of this size."

Virginia gave a little cry and jumped to her feet.

"Oh, Aunt Ella May," she said, throwing her arms round her aunt's neck, "I knew you would not fail me."

"It is all very well," her aunt said with a little laugh,

disentangling herself from the clinging arms, "but it is not going to be an easy task."

"You will write to him, will you not?" Virginia asked eagerly. "You will tell him that I want a divorce and that he can have any amount of money he likes as long as he sets me free?"

"I had not planned to do anything quite like that," her aunt said, walking into the kitchen.

"You had not?" Virginia asked as she followed her.

"To begin with," her aunt explained, "a man who is going to be asked to make such a momentous decision might be expected to come posting out here as soon as he received my letter. Do you really want that?"

Virginia's face paled.

"Of course I do not want him here," she said. "No, no, Aunt Ella May! You must keep him away. Tell him if he comes to America I will not give him a penny."

Her aunt put the peas into a small pan and added several pieces of golden butter.

"That will not work," she said firmly.

"Then what can we do?" Virginia asked despondently.

"I have an idea," Aunt Ella May said, busying herself at the stove. "I thought of it the other night and then I said to myself, 'No, that would not do for Virginia. She has not got the strength, for one thing, nor the determination for another.'"

"But, of course I have," Virginia asserted. "What is it?"

"I decided not even to speak about it," Aunt Ella May said. "You see, my idea needs somebody with strong determination, someone who is extremely intelligent, and someone who has got that delightful English word—'guts'. Honestly, Virginia darling, fond of you as I am, I do not think you qualify."

"Aunt Ella May, you insult me!" Virginia cried. "I have all those qualities, I have really. It is just that I have never been allowed to use them. Just give me the opportunity. I shall not fail you, I promise."

Her aunt turned from the stove with a faint smile on her lips.

"Very well, Virginia, I will tell you my plan. But hold your breath, because you are not going to like it."

"What is it?" Virginia asked, lifting her chin with a little, determined gesture that was new to her.

"It is," Aunt Ella May said in a quiet, matter-of-fact voice, "that you should go to England!"

3

VIRGINIA walked across the deck to stand at the stern of the ship, watching the smooth blue sea disturbed only by their wake and the sea-gulls swooping down with their plaintive cries. Many people watched her as she moved, the lovely, slim girl with the wonderful hair which seemed almost silver with golden lights in it.

Many of the men stared at her in admiration, but Virginia did not notice them. She was deep in her own thoughts, lost in a world that had no reality but the one on which her thoughts were centred.

It had taken a great deal of time and argument for her aunt to convince her that to go to England was the only possible thing for her to do.

"What is the alternative?" Aunt Ella May had asked. "For me to write to the Duke, to tell him you are better and to ask him to come out here to see you? Do you want that?"

Virginia shuddered.

"No," she said, "I could not bear him to come here. All the explanations, the astonishment at my changed appearance, and meeting him for the first time in a lawyer's office would somehow be intolerable. Can you not just write to him, Aunt Ella May, and tell him that I want a divorce?"

"I do not think he would give it to you, for one thing," Aunt Ella May replied. "You see, my love, I know the English aristocracy. They are very proud. They hate scandals. There is a great deal of what we, with our New England consciences, would call immorality amongst them, but husbands stick to their wives and wives to their husbands through thick and thin. However reprehensibly they behave in private, in public they keep up a united and certainly dignified appearance."

"Hypocrisy!" Virginia commented with scorn.

"In a way it is," Aunt Ella May agreed, "but there is something rather magnificent about them."

"How do you know all this?" Virginia asked curiously.

"When I first became a nurse," Aunt Ella May explained, "when we were quite poor—even your father—as a family, I got the very enviable post of being private nurse to Mr. Vanderbilt. He knew everyone and went everywhere, and he took me to England with him and we stayed at all the grand houses, including yours."

"Mine!" Virginia ejaculated.

"Yes, we stayed at Ryll Castle. Of course, your husband, the present Duke, was only a little boy—in fact, I do not remember even seeing him—but his father was a splendid man and his mother an aristocrat, though I never liked her."

"Did you talk to them?" Virginia asked.

Aunt Ella May laughed.

"I certainly did not presume to do that," she said, "but I saw them in the distance and I heard about them. Sometimes I was present when they conversed with Mr. Vanderbilt and it made a great impression on me. I want you to see for yourself what the way of life you are refusing is like."

"Can you see me in such circumstances?" Virginia asked with a little laugh.

"As a matter of fact I can," Aunt Ella May replied. "You are a very beautiful girl, Virginia, and the English appreciate beauty—especially a beautiful Duchess."

"Well, that is one thing they will never know about me," Virginia declared. "I accept your idea, Aunt Ella May, but only on condition that I go under a false name so that no one can possibly know who I am."

"I expect I have been reading too many novels," her aunt said with a little laugh, "but it seems to me a most exciting adventure. You set off, unknown, into the unknown. No one will recognise you because they have never seen you before. The Duke saw a fat monstrosity who bore your name, but why should he ever connect her with the slim, beautiful girl who visits Ryll Castle for a very different reason than to claim him as her husband?"

"Who do you suggest I should pretend to be?" Virginia asked. "That is, supposing I agree to your quite wild and crazy suggestion."

"I have thought it all out," Aunt Ella May said confidingly. "You told me yourself that you are interested in history. Well, when I reply to this last letter from the Duke I am going to ask him to do me a great favour. He cannot very well refuse, seeing that I am looking after his, supposedly, still unconscious wife. I shall say that I have a friend, a young girl who is studying English history, and I shall ask if, as a great condescension, he will allow her to come to Ryll Castle and put in some research in the magnificent library there."

"Is it really magnificent?" Virginia inquired.

"I only saw it once," Aunt Ella May replied, "when Mr. Vanderbilt sent me downstairs to get a book he wanted. But it was amazing. I often said to my husband, who loved books: 'If only you could see the library at Ryll Castle. It is too amazing to be believed.'"

"Do you think the Duke will agree to this suggestion?" Virginia asked. "Supposing he does not want an extra person at the Castle?"

Aunt Ella May threw back her head and laughed.

"Darling, he would not notice if I sent him an army. Ryll Castle is enormous. There must be hundreds, if not thousands, of people employed inside, in the stables, on the estates and in the forests. They even have their own brewery and carpenters' shop. I remember pushing Mr. Vanderbilt down to look at it because he was so interested."

"Could he not walk?" Virginia asked.

"Oh, no! He was a very old man when he employed me," Aunt Ella May answered, "and he chose me out of a whole lot of applicants because I was young. 'I like young people about me,' he used to say, 'they give me some of their youth.'"

Aunt Ella May gave a little sigh as if she half regretted the days that were past. Then she went on:

"Nothing you have ever seen in America will prepare you for England. But do not be too prejudiced against it. It has its good qualities as well as its bad and there is a pageant of social life which although not quite real is entrancing."

"Tell me more," Virginia urged. "Did you go to the parties?"

"No, of course I did not," Aunt Ella May replied. "I was only a nurse, looked on very much as a servant—a superior servant, but still a servant. However, because I had no pride, I used to peep over the banisters with the household staff when the Prince and Princess of Wales came to dinner. The ladies, in their low-cut evening dresses and bustles, with their tiaras, huge diamond necklaces and bracelets sparkling over their kid gloves, looked like beautiful swans. The men wore knee breeches and flashing decorations with such high collars that you would have thought they could hardly bend their heads. It was all very exciting and very glamorous. I used to wish that I could go downstairs and dance to the Viennese orchestra or flirt with one of the handsome young gentlemen in the conservatory."

"Aunt Ella May, I am surprised at you!" Virginia said.

"My dear, I was very romantic, otherwise I should not have married your uncle. It took a lot of courage to defy the whole family and walk out on all the inducements your father offered me to refuse him."

"You had more courage than I had," Virginia said in a low voice.

"My dear, you must not blame yourself. You were ill, very ill indeed."

"Dr. Fraser says that you saved my life," Virginia said.

"I think that if those city doctors had gone on treating you in that crazy fashion you would have died," her aunt agreed. "I blame them for a great deal of your illness, and the rest was your mother's fault."

"She did the best she could," Virginia said, instinctively going to the defence of her mother.

"She did what she thought was best for herself," Aunt Ella May replied. "I am sorry, Virginia, but you and I have always spoken frankly to each other and I think you have trusted me because I have always told you the truth. Your mother was a selfish woman and she forced you to make the greatest mistake any girl can make—to marry a man she did not love. I do not want you to make another mistake now."

"Do you mean that I should not get a divorce from the Duke?" Virginia asked.

"I think you have got to see for yourself what is the best way to end your marriage, if that is what you want," her aunt said gently.

"Of course that is what I want," Virginia protested. "Do you expect me to remain married to a fortune-hunter? A man who bought me as if I were some cheap purchase in a store? He sold his title to Mama and she handed me over, regardless of any feelings I might have in the matter."

"And she told him, of course, that you were averse to the marriage?" Aunt Ella May asked.

Virginia hesitated.

"No, I cannot imagine her doing that."

"Then how do you know that he was not marrying you believing, in all sincerity, that you wanted his title as much as he wanted your money? It might have been wrong; it might have been against what you and I think of as the decencies of human behaviour; but as a business deal it was perfectly legitimate on his part. From the average American point of view he was giving as good as he got."

"I had not thought of it like that," Virginia admitted.

"That is why, because I believe you to be a fair-minded creature and as fond of justice and personal freedom as I am, you should go to England and see for yourself. Find out a little bit about your husband's background. After all, we none of us know anything about him personally. Your mother claimed she was a friend of the old Duchess, which really meant she peeled out hundreds of dollars for some charity whenever the Duchess asked her to do so. And, incidentally, the Duchess extracted quite a lot of money from her. The solicitors sent your mother's personal correspondence here for me to sort through and to show you when you were well enough, and the Duchess was certainly not backward in asking. There was money for sick children; neglected animals; the 'down-and-outs'—or whatever they may be; the slum-dwellers; churches with spires about to topple down; and even a request for 'Comforts for Seamen'. It really astonishes me that anyone should ask people from another country to support their own national charities, but your mother obliged every time."

"She would never refuse a Duchess," Virginia laughed.

"That was evident," Aunt Ella May said drily, "and I dare say a lot of your money has now gone to support the same causes."

"What do you mean?" Virginia asked with rising interest.

"I mean that your husband can draw on your fortune as he pleases."

Virginia's lips tightened.

"In which case," she said, "I think it only right that I should go over and see how my money is being spent."

"That is exactly what I want you to do," her aunt agreed.

After that it became quite amusing to imagine herself going to England. It was fun going with her aunt to New York to buy clothes for the journey; fun to be able, for the first time, to indulge her own taste in dress and to find that everything she put on seemed to make her more attractive than she had ever imagined possible.

Her tiny waist, the sweet immaturity of her figure, made it easy for her to wear the dresses she had always imagined herself wearing—the soft, flowing chiffons, the tight bodices, the elegantly cut little boleros over a flowing skirt supported by a rustling silk petticoat.

She was wise enough not to buy anything flamboyant. As she said to her aunt:

"If I am to be an eager student of history I must not look too smart."

Aunt Ella May did not reply but her shrewd eyes noted that it did not matter what Virginia put on, it became a frame for her looks. Apart from her new, elegant figure she was also in fact much taller than she had been before.

"I have grown," Virginia had said the first time she saw herself in a long pier-glass.

"Exactly two and a half inches," her aunt said. "People often do when they are in bed for a long time."

"I cannot believe it," Virginia murmured—words she had repeated so often when looking at herself.

Also, since she had been up and out in the sunshine her hair had begun to lose its dead-white look. A touch of gold was creeping into it so that at times it looked silver, at other times the colour of the first rays of the morning sun.

Every day her aunt instructed Virginia in the etiquette of living in English houses.

"Of course, I have never been in the grand Salons or even in the dining-room," Aunt Ella May said wistfully. "But I know a great deal of the behaviour from hearing Mr. Vanderbilt and his family talk. For instance, the most important lady always leaves the room first after dinner and then the others follow according to their status."

"And supposing you do not know how important the other people are?" Virginia asked.

"Then you go last," her aunt said with a laugh. "It is far better to be thought humble than pushing."

There were so many things to remember that after a time Virginia said:

"Well, I guess I had better just be myself. They will just think I am an American and that I do not know any better. Besides, as you say, I shall not be in the grand part of the house, so what does it matter?"

"You might get invited to dinner when there is nobody important there," Aunt Ella May said hopefully, but Virginia knew that her aunt was only trying to console her and it was most unlikely.

"They are a lot of stuck-up snobs," Virginia muttered to herself when she was alone. "I will go and look at them, just so that when I get home I can be thankful for what I have missed."

But when the moment came to depart she was frightened.

"I do not want to go, Aunt Ella May. I have changed my mind. Let me stay with you."

"Chicken-hearted!" her aunt taunted her. "That does not sound very American to me."

"Why should I go over to England and be patronised by people whom I hate and despise?" Virginia asked passionately, thinking of the Duke.

"Do not let them patronise you," Aunt Ella May replied. "Stick your chin out at them—that nice little Virginian chin which I have noticed you can use quite effectively when you want to get your own way!"

Virginia laughed, she could not help it.

"You are ridiculous, Aunt Ella May!"

"Do you know, I remember you as a little girl falling off your pony," her aunt said. "You must have been about eight at the time, and when your father ran up to console you you said: 'Put me up on him again. I am not going to be defeated by him—not if he kicks me off a dozen times!'"

"Did I really say that?" Virginia smiled.

"I was so impressed by it at the time," Aunt Ella May said. "I thought to myself, that child will never be defeated by life."

"And you are determined that I shall not be defeated now, are you not?" Virginia said. "Well, I do not care, I will tell you the truth. I am frightened."

"You will not be frightened when you get there," her aunt said consolingly. "Remember, you are not in the least important. It is doubtful whether anyone will even notice you. Most English people think America is full of Red Indians and millionaires. They have no interest in the people who come betwixt and between."

"And I shall be a betwixt and between," Virginia said. "I will remember that and be suitably unobtrusive."

"Do not miss anything," her aunt admonished. "I want to hear all about it, every single detail. Oh, Virginia! If only I were young enough I would come with you."

"Why not?" Virginia asked. "Come now!"

"And what would happen to all my animals? My chickens, my cows, my garden? No, I am too old to go

41

gallivanting. But I went once, and now if you go I shall be happy at home."

"And that is what I shall be able to say in a few months," Virginia said.

Her aunt did not answer, but when she came aboard the liner to see Virginia off she held her very close.

"God take care of you, my dear," she said. "I only pray that I have done the right thing in sending you off on this great adventure."

"There is still time for me to get off the ship before she sails," Virginia said.

"And waste all those expensive clothes!" her aunt protested. "Shame on you, Virginia! You know as well as I do that they were bought for a special purpose. It would be quite immoral to use them for anything else."

Virginia, who had been very near tears, dissolved into laughter.

"Oh, Aunt Ella May, you do say the most absurd things," she said. "Thank you for the flowers."

She looked at the big bunch of roses standing on the dressing-table in her cabin.

"I sent some to Mrs. Winchester in your name," Aunt Ella May said, "so do not be surprised when she thanks you."

"Is she in the next cabin?" Virginia asked.

"I think she is a little way down the passage," her aunt replied, "because she is sharing a cabin. She is the wife of an American and she is obviously not very well off. So do not forget, Virginia, you must pay for things when you can. She will not be able to afford any luxuries."

"But as she is chaperoning me why did you not pay for her passage across the Atlantic?" Virginia asked.

"Well, would that not seem very queer from a young student of history who, although she has a little money of her own, cannot afford to splash it about as if she were a Rockefeller?"

Virginia laughed again.

"I keep forgetting," she said.

"Think yourself into the part," her aunt warned her. "I always remember when we used to act at college our producer used to say: 'Believe you are Julius Caesar and you will be him! Believe you are Cleopatra and with a great deal of make-up you may look like her.' "

"I am Virginia Langholme, history student travelling to England for the purposes of research," Virginia recited.

"And I hope, later, that I may write a special book on the subject."

"You are the prettiest history student who ever came out of America," her aunt said.

"I still think it was a mistake to call me 'Virginia'."

"Oh, we have been over this before," Aunt Ella May exclaimed. "Why on earth should the Duke connect Virginia Langholme with his wife whom he believes to be in a coma and not yet to have regained consciousness? There are thousands of girls in America called Virginia. And do not forget, all he has to remember you by are newspaper cuttings."

Virginia shivered.

"I hate even to think about it," she said. "That great mountain of flesh lying on the floor."

"Well, then, do not agitate yourself," her aunt said. "He would not recognise you in ten million years. It might be worth telling him before you come home just to see the astonishment on his face!"

"As if I should be likely to do anything of the sort!" Virginia said scornfully. "No, Aunt Ella May. This is a voyage of exploration. There will be no dramatic announcements and certainly no happy ending at the conclusion of it."

"No?" her aunt said enigmatically. "Englishmen, as a whole, can be very attractive."

"When I am free," Virginia declared, "I am going to find myself an attractive American just like Uncle Clement, and we will go and live on a little farm, like you, and forget all about my money and be happy ever after."

"I only hope that is a true prophecy," Aunt Ella May said. "But from what I have seen of your fellow passengers you are not going to find him on this ship."

"I hope not," Virginia replied.

Her aunt had been right about the other passengers. They were a dull lot—businessmen who spent most of their time in the bar, cracking jokes which brought uproarious shouts of laughter; old people taking the voyage for the benefit of their health; and others, like Mrs. Winchester, an American whose husband worked in London and who was rejoining him after a short visit to her relatives in Ohio.

Mrs. Winchester was a talkative woman who liked the sound of her own voice, but to Virginia's relief she felt seasick soon after the ship left New York harbour and retired to her cabin. The weather was a bit choppy for the first two days but after that it was fine and warm. All the English people aboard had only one topic of conversation—the weather.

"I always think August is the best time for travelling," Virginia would hear them say, over and over again.

And their greeting to each other was invariably the same:

"Nice day!"

"Yes, isn't it!"

One or two people made tentative approaches to talk to her, to get her to join in the ship's games and to ask her what she thought about the weather. But, while she was polite, she made it quite clear that she wanted to be alone. There was so much that she wanted to consider: not only what lay ahead but also about herself.

It seemed to her that recovering from her illness had been like being re-born. It was almost as if in that long year when she was unconscious she had gone back to being in an embryo state and then been born into a world that was entirely new, a world that had really nothing in common with the one she had known previously.

All the time, in her secret heart, there was a wild elation at the thought of being free. "I am free! I am free!" she kept telling herself; free of her mother's domination; free, for the moment, of the responsibilities and trouble that her fortune had brought her; free even from her own worries and anxieties about her future. The ship was like a vehicle out of time carrying her from yesterday to tomorrow, and for the moment relieving her of everything that had thwarted her or made her unhappy in the past.

When the coast of England came in sight she had a strange feeling that she was a conqueror about to discover a new and unknown land. She felt excited and no longer afraid. She was alone and yet she was not lonely. For the first time in her life there was no one to stop her doing anything she wished.

When she set foot in England she could disappear, if she desired, and no one would know where she had gone. She could go from England to the Continent or, if she pleased, she could return immediately to America. She felt as if she had shed the last shrinkings of anxiety about the future like a discarded skin and was now emerging with wings.

She had reached England and England was an adventure greater than anything she had undertaken before.

She ran down to her cabin to pack her things. In the passage she met Mrs. Winchester, still looking pale and wan after the voyage.

"Oh, Miss Langholme!" she said. "I have been looking for you to apologise. I feel so terrible that I have not been able to look after you all through the voyage, but I felt so ill, so desperately ill. In fact, the doctor says he has never had a patient suffer as much as I have. I assure you, Miss Langholme, that I detest the sea. As I said to the doctor, 'I would rather swim to America than go through this again!'"

"I am sorry for you, Mrs. Winchester," Virginia said, "but please do not worry about me. I have been perfectly capable of looking after myself."

"I feel real ashamed of myself at not being able to do more for you. But now you are in England you will be all right, will you not? You have people meeting you, I expect?"

"Yes, yes," Virginia said immediately. "There will be people meeting me. Please do not worry about me, Mrs. Winchester." Her one idea was to get rid of the old gossip.

Mrs. Winchester followed her into her cabin, repeating herself over and over again, saying how sorry she was and how she would write to her aunt to apologise.

"Oh, please do not worry Aunt Ella May," Virginia said. "I shall tell her that we got on splendidly. It would only agitate her if you said anything to the contrary."

"Then we will keep it just a secret to ourselves," Mrs. Winchester said. "When you come to London you must visit me. You are going to the country first, I think."

"Yes, to the country," Virginia repeated, determined that Mrs. Winchester should not know her real destination.

"Then here is my address," Mrs. Winchester said, handing her a slip of paper. "My husband and I will be pleased to welcome you. We have only a small house provided for him by our organisation, but there is a guest room, if you do not mind it being in the attic, and we shall be real glad, always, to see you."

"It is very kind of you," Virginia said. "Thank you very much. And thank you for your chaperonage. It was extremely kind of you to say that you would look after me."

"And yet I feel I have failed lamentably in my duty," Mrs. Winchester said, starting all over again.

It was with difficulty that Virginia got rid of her and started her packing. She placed all her new dresses carefully in her round-topped trunks, called the cabin-steward to fasten the straps and tied on to the handles the labels that Aunt Ella May had already neatly written out for her:

Miss Virginia Langholme, passenger to Ryll Castle, Kent.

Virginia had not really expected anyone to meet her, but as she came down the gangway a very superior, elderly man, carrying a bowler hat, came forward and said:

"Miss Virginia Langholme?"

"Yes, I am Miss Langholme," Virginia replied.

"I am instructed by His Grace the Duke of Merrill to escort you to the train," he said. "The carriage is waiting. Already I have porters collecting your luggage."

Virginia was led to a very comfortable carriage and from there taken to the railway station. The elderly man produced her ticket and she found that a whole first-class carriage had been reserved for her. There was a foot-warmer for her feet, and a large picnic basket was set down opposite her.

"I hope you will have everything you want, miss," the elderly man said respectfully. "I will come along when the train stops at the junction and see if there is anything else you require."

"It is very kind of His Grace to take so much trouble," Virginia said.

"You are a guest at the Castle, miss," the elderly man said almost in tones of rebuke.

Virginia gave a little smile as he walked away and as soon as the train started, she opened the hamper with an almost childlike curiosity. She could never have imagined a more elaborate or luxurious picnic. There was *pâté de foie gras*; a dish of quail; a wing of chicken set in aspic and ornamented with various little delicacies. There were profiteroles filled with cream; three sorts of cheese; a pat of golden butter inscribed with the Ducal crest. There were fresh rolls, biscuits and toast; a profusion of fruit—huge peaches as large as tennis balls, muscat grapes, and golden-skinned pears. To drink there was a bottle of hock, one of water and a silver flask filled with coffee and wrapped in flannel.

"If this is a sample of the meals at Ryll Castle," Virginia

told herself, "I shall soon be as fat as I was a year ago."

She ate a little chicken and enjoyed some fruit. The bottle of hock remained unopened and, remembering that her aunt had never approved of the American habit of imbibing unlimited cups of coffee, she left the flask untouched.

"I am too excited to be hungry," Virginia thought to herself, and began to count the hours until they arrived at Ryll. There was a carriage waiting at the small, wayside station at which the train made a special stop. A board on the tiny platform read: *Ryll Castle Only*.

As she stepped out the elderly man was already instructing a porter to remove the luggage from the guard's van. She turned towards the exit. Outside the station there was a pair of magnificent black horses drawing a closed brougham. They were tossing their heads disdainfully, as if annoyed at being kept waiting, and as they did so their silver bridles jangled and flashed in the evening sunshine. There was both a coachman and a footman on the box.

Virginia stepped in and waited for the elderly courier who had escorted her to join her. The door was shut. Hastily she let down the window. The man was standing outside, his bowler hat held respectfully in his hand.

"Are you not coming with me?" she asked.

"Oh, no, miss!" he replied. "I have now completed my instructions."

"Then, goodbye! And thank you very much!" Virginia said.

"It has been a pleasure," he said in an almost courtly tone and bowed as the brougham moved away.

"Well," Virginia said to herself, sinking back against the cushioned seats, "His Grace certainly does things in style. If he treats a chance student in this manner, what would be laid on for a Duchess?"

She smiled to herself at the thought. There was something rather fascinating about being incognito in the interior of what she thought of as the "lion's den".

In a very short time she realised they had entered the drive of Ryll Castle. There were huge oaks on either side of it and then, after a few moments, she had her first sight of the home of the man she had married. She could not help drawing in her breath in a quite audible gasp.

Silhouetted against the sunlit sky Ryll Castle was a fantastic sight. Its turrets and towers had an almost fairy-like quality, and at the same time it was so enormous that she felt it could not, in fact, be a private residence. As she gazed at it, while the horses carried her sedately up the drive, she saw a sudden flight of white doves circling over the roofs and a flag fluttered out in the evening breeze. It was almost as if the castle was welcoming her, and she knew she would have been very insensitive if she had not been stirred by the sight of this great edifice standing majestically on what appeared to be a slight incline, dwarfing with its very magnificence the gardens and woods which encircled it.

She had a fleeting glimpse of a lake and on its mirrored surface swans, black and white, and a number of colourful ducks.

"It is lovely!" Virginia whispered to herself, and almost before she was ready the horses came to a standstill. She saw a flight of steps and a footman, in dark green livery with silver-crested buttons, hurrying down to open the carriage door.

She stepped out. At the top of the steps there were enormous double doors, oak and studded with great nails. One of them was open.

As she started to climb the steps, two men came hurrying through the front door in such haste that it was almost as if they were propelled. And after them came a tall dark man, shouting in a furious voice:

"Get out and stay there! If ever I find you in this house again I shall wring your necks for you! Do you hear me?"

"But . . . the Duchess . . . asked us . . ." one of the men managed to stammer, his face pale with fear.

"Whatever Her Grace did or did not do," came the answer, "you will obey my command. Get out and never come back! If you do, it will be the worse for you both. Now go!"

There was so much fury and venom in his tone that the two men—Virginia guessed them to be tradesmen of some sort—recoiled at the sound of it and one of them half fell down the steps.

She stood paralysed, unable to move, wondering what she should do. But already the man who had cursed them had disappeared and now a butler, white-haired and looking uncommonly like a bishop, appeared in the doorway.

"Miss Virginia Langholme, I believe?" he said, in quiet, respectful tones. "Will you come this way, ma'am."

With an effort Virginia forced herself to walk up the steps.

"Who . . . who was that?" she asked, and the butler made no effort to misunderstand her.

"His Grace is a little incensed today," he said soothingly.

"Incensed!" Virginia repeated, then checked herself.

It was not for her to criticise her host. But that—that was her husband!

4

A FOOTMAN, resplendent in green and silver and over six feet tall, escorted Virginia up the grand staircase. As soon as he was out of earshot of the butler she noticed that he relaxed, and was conscious immediately of her class status in this aristocratic household.

"You come from America don't you, miss?" the footman asked.

"Yes," Virginia answered. "I arrived at Southampton this morning."

"I have often wondered about America," the footman confided. "I never thought there were people like you, miss. I thought the whole country was full of Red Indians and millionaires!"

He laughed at his own joke and Virginia realised that because the household knew she was only an American interested in research in the library and not a proper guest they could treat her with this friendly informality. She was not annoyed by it, only amused, and when an obviously under under-housemaid came to unpack for her the girl was as chatty as the footman had been.

"I hope you'll like it here, miss," she said, taking Virginia's new clothes out of the trunk and hanging them in the big wardrobe. "But I expect it will seem strange to you after America."

"Why should it?" Virginia asked curiously.

"Oh, well, you're different from us over there, aren't you?" the housemaid explained. "And I don't suppose you have houses like this, not even for the millionaires we hear so much about."

"No, we have big houses, but not exactly like this," Virginia said.

She had been impressed almost despite herself by the beauty inside the Castle. The great, curving, oak staircase with its carved newels of cupids was magnificent. She knew enough about pictures to realise that everywhere she looked there were fine examples not only of the English school but of the Italian Renaissance, of Flemish and Dutch artists, and she was even delighted to recognise a famous Van Dyck that she had seen in her art books.

Her bedroom was comfortable and attractive, but small as befitted her position. The bathroom, when she had ascertained its whereabouts, was, as she had expected, a long way down the corridor. She was, however, fascinated by everything and stood for a long time looking out of her window to the lake below and across it to the great trees in the park which must have stood there for hundreds of years.

In the centre of the lake there was a little island and she saw that on it was built something which looked like a Grecian temple. She felt herself itching to explore everything: the rose-gardens which she could vaguely see were at the corner of the house; the woods in the distance; and the stables which she had noticed when they drove up to the Castle and which were tucked away beside the west wing.

It was all fascinating and she forgot for a moment the reason why she had come to England. She just felt a thrill of exploring something new, of entering a world of which she knew little and which she anticipated would be full of surprises.

She changed from her travelling-dress into a thin gown of flowered muslin. It was very simply made and yet it had been a very expensive model which she had bought on Fifth Avenue. Now, when she looked in her mirror, she was glad she had been extravagant.

The white muslin patterned with small flowers and the draped chiffon fichu round her shoulders made her look absurdly young and yet very attractive. She would have been a liar if she had not admitted that her strangely silvered hair made her look different from other women and would draw the eyes of any beholder. She had refused, against Aunt Ella May's advice, to go to some expensive hairdresser and be shown the very latest mode of hairdressing. Instead, she swept it to the back of her head and knotted it low at the nape of her neck. It was so buoyant and full of vitality as it framed her little face, giving her what seemed an almost living halo and a look of classical elegance.

She was just ready when there came a knock at the door.

"Come in!" she called, and the door opened to reveal a middle-aged woman wearing pince-nez and a severely cut coat and skirt of white serge.

"I am Marjorie Marshbanks!" she said in an intensely cultured voice. "Secretary to Her Grace. I came along to see if I could help you in any way."

"How very kind of you," Virginia said. "I am Virginia Langholme, as, of course, you know, and I have been most courteously looked after ever since I stepped off the ship."

"We do our best to make our guests feel at home," Miss Marshbanks said in a prim voice. "Now I expect you would like a cup of tea. Will you come downstairs with me and I will show you where our own little sitting-room is, and afterwards I will take you up to meet Her Grace."

Virginia picked up her handbag. It was rather heavy and cumbersome to carry but she did not like to leave it behind seeing that she had not yet found anywhere she could lock away the quite considerable sum of money she had brought with her.

"Of course," Aunt Ella May had said, "you can have money sent to a bank in England, but it might lead to explanations. I think the best thing is for you to take quite a lot with you. If you run short you can always cable me and then I can make arrangements with the trustees."

"I do not want the trustees to know where I am," Virginia said quickly.

"I know," Aunt Ella May said. "That is why I have drawn the money for you out of my own bank."

"You will not be short, will you?" Virginia asked.

"No, of course not," her aunt smiled. "If I want anything I have only got to say it is for you. But in the meantime it gives me rather a thrill to be financing you. It is not without its humour when you think about it. The poverty-stricken widow of an unsuccessful farmer, playing banker to my very, very wealthy niece!"

"When I come back we will admit that I am alive," Virginia said, "and I am going to buy you the most wonderful farm in the whole of America."

"You will do nothing of the sort," her aunt said tartly. "I would not move from here if you offered me the Shah of Persia's Palace! And the strange thing is, which nobody would believe, I have got everything I want. There is nothing you can give me, Virginia, except your love."

"And that you have got already," Virginia cried, kissing her. "You are all my family now, you know that, father, mother, brothers, sisters, cousins and aunts. If any other relatives exist, I do not wish to see them. You are all I have and all I want to have."

"You will make me cry if you talk like that," Aunt Ella May said, and indeed there was a suspicion of tears in her eyes.

As Virginia picked up her handbag she thought that she would guard Aunt Ella May's money even more carefully than she would guard her own. "I expect there is a drawer that will lock," she thought, "and I will put it in inconspicuous envelopes so that if anyone does look in the drawer they will not realise it is money."

Miss Marshbanks was chattering gaily.

"I am really very interested to meet you," she said. "I have often thought of being a librarian myself, but, there, I never have the time. The Duchess keeps me on the run day and night, and I can assure you that is literally true when we have one of our big parties here, such as we used to have frequently when the late Duke was alive. Royalty always in the shooting season, and they come for the best part of a week at other times of the year. And what with their ladies-in-waiting and their valets, maids, couriers and coachmen, it all takes a lot of arranging I can tell you."

"And do you organise it all?" Virginia asked, knowing that was the right question.

"But, of course, my dear. The Duchess trusts me absolutely. How often has she said to me: 'I do not know what I should do without you, Marshy'—that is what they call me, you know! A little term of affection which the present Duke invented when he was small."

"The house is so big it must take a lot of running," Virginia observed.

"Of course, the servants have been here for years," Miss Marshbanks explained. "Not that that is always an advantage, between you and me. Sometimes they get above themselves. But it does make for things running smoothly in the household. It is the guests who are the difficulty, Oh dear! If you only knew the trouble I have about placing them in the right rooms."

She laughed gaily as Virginia looked puzzled.

"I see you do not understand what I am talking about. Well, my dear, when you have been in England long enough you will realise that in Society there is one word that matters and that is 'tact'. You see, if a very charming gentleman is enamoured, shall we say, of a certain very charming lady, then it might be a tragedy if one of them was put on one floor and the other on another!"

"You mean . . ." Virginia began.

"Exactly what I say," Miss Marshbanks interposed. "Of course, that sort of gaffe does not happen at Ryll, I can assure you, because the Duchess and I are very certain to see that it does not."

By this time they had reached a small sitting-room tucked away on the ground floor down a long passage. It was a charming room, complete with piano, a comfortable sofa and several armchairs.

"My office is upstairs near Her Grace," Miss Marshbanks explained. "But this is where I relax if ever I have the time to do so, and where I have my meals. I had the table put in the window. It is most pleasant to look out on to the gardens on a sunny day."

"It must be quite delightful," Virginia said.

"And the food is good here," Miss Marshbanks went on. "Very good. Not like some houses I could name, where the secretary is fed worse than the superior servants. I would not stand for that sort of thing and the staff here know it. I should go straight to Her Grace and report any shortcoming in my menu. The chef, by this time, knows my likes and dislikes. You must tell me if there are any special dishes you favour."

"I do not eat an awful lot," Virginia said.

"I can see that," Miss Marshbanks replied. "We shall have to fatten you up. If you will forgive my saying so, you are very thin. I pride myself that I never drop much below eleven stone."

"And you feel well at that weight?" Virginia said, striving mentally to turn English stones into American pounds.

"My dear Miss Langholme, the most important thing is for me to keep my health," Miss Marshbanks explained. "If I were not here the whole place would be chaos. The Duchess, I assure you, is just a child when it comes to finance, to housekeeping or to arranging any of the hundreds of little things that have to be seen to in the Castle day after day. No, it is Marshy who does it, as you will find out for yourself when you have been here a few days."

A footman brought in an elegant tea. There were several different sorts of bread-and-butter, tiny freshly baked scones, rolled bread containing asparagus tips and three different kinds of cake.

"Now, you must be hungry after that long journey," Miss Marshbanks said. "So do not stand on ceremony, just tuck in, as the Duke used to say when he was a small boy."

Virginia ate a piece of bread-and-butter but felt herself quite unable to do justice to the cakes. Miss Marshbanks, however, sampled everything and Virginia was not surprised that her weight was more than it should have been. She remembered what all the cakes and cookies and rich pudding that she had eaten in the past had done to her and shuddered.

"You are not cold, are you?" Miss Marshbanks asked. "It seems very warm today, but your dress is thin. I hope you brought some thicker clothes with you. It will soon be autumn and then I assure you it can be really chilly."

"Yes, I brought some thicker clothes," Virginia replied, "but I shall not be staying very long."

"You will not?" Miss Marshbanks raised her eyebrows. "Her Grace gave me to understand that the letter the Duke received from America said you were working on some very important research."

"Yes, I am," Virginia agreed, "but I do not think it will entail my staying very long in one place."

She had a sudden feeling that in talking to Miss Marshbanks she was sinking into a warm feather-bed and soon it would be difficult to exert herself to rise out of it.

"Well, if you have finished," Miss Marshbanks said, eating the last crumb of a heavy fruit-cake, "we had better be going up to see Her Grace. She always rests about this time. She will be in her *boudoir*. I told her I would bring you along."

They went up the beautiful staircase. Virginia promised herself that somehow she would find time to inspect every picture, look at every piece of furniture in the hall and along the corridor. She realised they were all treasures and quite unlike any of the expensive and elaborate objects with which her mother had cluttered the house on Fifth Avenue or the other half a dozen houses her father had owned. And the sense of age gave a bloom to the whole place, just as the slightly faded red velvet curtains were more beautiful now than they had been in their pristine freshness.

Miss Marshbanks knocked on a door. A faint voice spoke and they entered. It was not a large room and for a moment Virginia thought it was not unlike one of her mother's drawing-rooms; the tables everywhere held huge vases of hot-house flowers and innumerable little silver ornaments. There was a great deal of Dresden china, and the chairs and the couch were piled with silk cushions of every shape and colour.

The Duchess was resting on a day-bed by the window and Virginia's first impression was that she was much younger than she had expected. Then, as she drew nearer, she saw it was an illusion which was due to the fact that the Duchess's face was powdered and there was a faint suspicion of colour on her lips. She was dressed in a diaphanous, mauve tea-gown of pleated chiffon slotted with velvet ribbons and trimmed with lace. She wore three long rows of enormous pearls and there were diamonds sparkling in her ears and in the bracelets encircling her thin wrists.

"What is it, Marshy?" she asked in a somewhat petulant voice.

"I have brought Miss Virginia Langholme to see you, Your Grace," Miss Marshbanks replied. "You remember she was arriving today from America?"

"Oh, yes, of course!"

The Duchess half sat up in her interest and held out her hand in quite an easy fashion.

"It is very kind of you to have me," Virginia said.

"We are delighted, are we not, Marshy? Absolutely delighted! That great big library is empty year after year and I do not believe anyone ever opens a book."

"Oh, indeed, Your Grace!" Miss Marshbanks protested. "I read."

"Rubbish!" the Duchess said. "You know quite well the books in the library are far too dull for you. You like a slushy, lurid romance. You cannot pretend that your bedroom is not full of them!"

"Oh, Your Grace!" Miss Marshbanks cried, flushing a little, but Virginia could see that she was pleased at being teased.

"Now run away, Marshy. I want to talk to Miss

Langholme. I want to hear all about my friends in America," the Duchess said, and rather reluctantly Miss Marshbanks withdrew from the *boudoir*.

The Duchess lay back against the cushions and motioned Virginia to sit in the chair at her side. She could see now that there were lines around Her Grace's eyes and no cosmetics could disguise the fact that her jaw had begun to sag a little. Her hair, dressed in the very latest fashion on top of her head, waving back from her oval forehead, was a very elegant shade of red and showed no signs of encroaching greyness.

"Now, tell me all about America," the Duchess demanded. "I used to have some very dear friends there—one in particular, who was most kind to me whenever I needed money, for my charities, of course. Her name was Mrs. Stuyvesant Clay. I wonder if you ever came across her?"

Virginia, rather nonplussed, was wondering how to lie convincingly, when the Duchess chattered on:

"No, of course you would not have. She lived in New York and was very rich, very rich indeed. I miss her! I suppose you are not rich, Miss Langholme?"

Again, before Virginia could answer, the Duchess continued:

"But why should you be? I think my son said you were a student or something. It is just that Americans always seem to be rich, and generous as well. By the way, were there not two gentlemen at the station when you arrived who would have accompanied you to the castle?"

"No, there was no one," Virginia said.

"I cannot understand it," the Duchess said. "I had an appointment with them for this afternoon. They never arrived."

Virginia was wondering whether she should mention the drama at the front door when the Duchess continued:

"If you were rich it would be so very helpful. There is something . . . something very important for which I need money at the moment."

"A lot of money?" Virginia asked.

"A lot," the Duchess said with a sigh. "But even a little would be something to be going on with. You could not help me, could you? I do not like to ask this of you, but even five pounds would be a tremendous help."

Virginia was completely taken aback by this strange

request, but telling herself that she should be surprised at nothing she said:

"I think I could manage . . . five pounds, if it would help Your Grace."

"You could!" the Duchess's eyes sparkled. "Then let me have it now if you can."

Virginia opened her bag. Fortunately, she had put a few sovereigns in her purse while the rest of her money was hidden in other compartments. She had changed her American dollars little by little on the ship, taking care they should not realise at one time how much money she had with her. Now she took out five bright gold sovereigns and passed them over to the Duchess.

"Thank you! Thank you very much indeed, my dear! It is very kind of you," the Duchess said. "It really will be a help."

"You say that Mrs. Stuyvesant Clay used to help your charities?" Virginia said, remembering the list that Aunt Ella May had read out to her.

"My . . . my charities! Oh, yes—of course!" the Duchess replied. "A very kind woman. It is a great pity she is dead. As a matter of fact . . ."

She was going to say more when the door opened and Virginia felt herself stiffen as the Duke came into the room. Now she was able to look at him and she saw that he was, indeed, extremely good-looking; but there was a grim expression on his face and he was frowning as he approached his mother.

"Oh, Sebastian, there you are!" the Duchess exclaimed. "I was wondering why you had not been to see me."

"I was kept from doing so," the Duke replied. "Were you expecting two visitors?"

The Duchess flushed and for a moment Virginia could see she was intending to deny the accusation. Then she said almost defiantly:

"Yes, I was! Do you know what has happened to them?"

"I have told them that, if they ever come here again," the Duke said slowly, "I will wring their necks!"

"You have sent them away!" the Duchess said with a little cry.

"I have sent them away," he repeated. "You know as well as I do, Mother, that you have nothing to sell."

"But I was only going to let them look at one or two of

my things," the Duchess said almost apologetically.

"Do you mean your jewellery?" the Duke asked. "You have none of your own. I have told you over and over again, Mother, that what you are wearing are heirlooms. You sold what belonged to you ages ago. If anyone buys what you offer them now, they are committing a legal offence and can be prosecuted."

"I do not understand it," the Duchess said in a sudden petulance. "And it is absolutely intolerable that people, whoever they may be, who call to see me should be sent away without my even being informed."

"I am sorry, Mother, but I have given Matthews instructions that if he ever lets that type of person into the Castle again he will lose his job."

"Matthews lose his job! He has been here nearly forty years!" the Duchess cried. "You must be insane! Really, Sebastian, you overstep yourself. I will not have you behaving in this way. I am not a child nor a lunatic that you should treat me in such an autocratic manner."

"I treat you, I hope, with the utmost respect and affection," the Duke replied. "But I will not allow you to sell the family heirlooms so that you can gamble away the money, night after night. And why should you need money? You promised me that you would not play for high stakes. You gave me your solemn word on that account. I cannot believe you are in debt."

The Duchess's eyes flickered.

"No, of course I am not, you stupid boy! And please stop talking to me of such personal matters, and let me introduce you to our guest from America."

The Duke started, stared at Virginia, and his expression changed. From concentrating almost fiercely upon his mother, he said apologetically:

"Forgive me, I did not realise there was a stranger present. I thought you were Miss Marshbanks."

The Duchess gave a little scream of laughter.

"She does not look much like Marshy, does she? And she is a charming girl. I hope she will enjoy working here."

The Duke held out his hand and Virginia found herself rising a little unsteadily to her feet.

"I hope too, as my mother said, that you will enjoy working here," he said, and a smile completely transformed his face.

"I am sure it will be very interesting," Virginia replied, and tried not to feel shy and embarrassed.

There was something unreal in touching the hand of the man to whom she was married, in knowing he was looking at her with a little glint of admiration in his eyes and that the smile on his lips was very friendly.

"I am sure you will forgive me for my apparent rudeness," he said. "Perhaps you will allow me to take you downstairs and show you the library—that is if you have not seen it already."

For a moment Virginia wanted to refuse and then she thought it would be discourteous.

"It is very kind of you," she murmured.

"A good idea," the Duchess approved. "And now I must have my rest. Do not be angry with me, Sebastian. I have done no wrong."

"Only because I prevented it," the Duke answered ruefully.

"It was a mistake," the Duchess said airily. "Let us forget about it."

The Duke gave a sigh and moved across the room to open the door for Virginia. They went down the staircase in silence and she knew he was still preoccupied with his mother. Then, with an effort, he started to explain to her the history of the Castle—when it was built, first in the Norman times, added to in the reign of Henry VIII, and that a portion of it had been burned down in the eighteenth century and his father had spent a great deal of money in adding a further wing about thirty years ago.

"It is a pot-pourri of each succeeding generation," he said. "Of course, the first Rylls lived here. It was Charles I who knighted Sir Thomas Ryll for services to the Crown. We became Earls in the reign of Queen Anne and the Dukedom followed at the time of George IV."

"It is very interesting," Virginia said, watching the Duke as he talked and realising that the history of his family meant something to him. There was a note in his voice that told her he paid not just lip-service to the past but that the Castle and all it contained was near and dear to him.

There was a puzzled look on her face as finally they came to the library and the Duke flung open the door with a flourish.

"Here are many of the most priceless treasures in the whole house," he said.

Aunt Ella May had told her that the library was beautiful, but she had not expected anything so large or perfectly proportioned. There were books rising from the floor to the ceiling, which was arched and painted with a magnificent panorama of gods and goddesses. There were long windows set with patterns of stained glass which let in the sunshine and threw a kaleidoscope of colour upon the floor. There was a gallery running round half the room which was served by a small, curving staircase, and everywhere one looked there were books—books exquisitely bound in tooled leather in soft, warm colours which, blending one into another, seemed to make a pattern for the walls more beautiful than anything that could have been devised by a painter.

"It is fantastic!" Virginia said and clasped her hands together.

"I thought you would think so," the Duke said. "Whenever I come back to it, having been away, I think there is no room like it and no place I would rather be. You will enjoy working here. There is your desk," he pointed to one in the middle of the room—"and there is a rather inadequate and very out-of-date catalogue. I only hope you will be able to find what you want."

"I am sure I shall," Virginia answered.

But having shown her the library the Duke did not go. Instead, he leaned against the mantelpiece and said:

"You are not at all what I expected!"

Virginia flushed.

"What did you expect?" she asked.

"A blue-stocking," he answered. "An earnest young woman with glasses and pimples—they always seem to go together!"

"Oh, that is unfair!" Virginia expostulated.

"Well, I take back the pimples," the Duke said, "but certainly someone who looked very erudite."

"You do not always have to look what you are," Virginia smiled.

"You say that as if it had a special meaning," the Duke replied.

Virginia looked away. "He is more perceptive than I thought," she told herself. "I shall have to be careful."

"I was but stating a general fact," she said aloud.

"I hope sometimes you will let me come and talk to you," the Duke said. "I find there are very few people who read these days, and especially not young women."

"Perhaps you are unfortunate in your acquaintances," Virginia suggested.

"Perhaps," he answered, "and that is all the more reason why I should like talking to you."

"I am afraid I shall be too busy for much conversation," she said. "I have a great deal of work to do in a very short space of time."

"Why the hurry?" he asked. "Surely while you are here you want to see England? It is rather a beautiful island. You must not miss all our historical sights in London."

"I doubt if I shall be able to go there," Virginia said.

"Everyone seems in such a hurry these days," the Duke sighed. "I think sometimes they miss a lot. Very soon we shall have hundreds of this new-fangled vehicle, the motor-car, tearing down our roads and lanes, creating a tremendous dust and giving people no time to see the beauties of the countryside."

Speaking with feeling in his voice, he walked across to one of the windows and opened it. Virginia watched him with a perplexed expression on her face.

"Come here," he said.

Virginia obeyed him. He opened wide the window and she looked out over a different part of the grounds from that she had seen before. There were long herbaceous borders stretching away to where, in the distance, a fountain was playing, its water iridescent against the sky. And beyond that there was a vista of trees and shrubs stretching towards a misty horizon where a great wood was dark against the golden glow of the setting sun.

"It is very beautiful!" Virginia said.

"Everywhere you look around Ryll you will find beauty," the Duke said. "But I mean to make it more beautiful still. When you are looking through the books here, if you come across the old Elizabethan plans of the gardens will you tell me at once? I know they are somewhere in this room but although I have searched I cannot find them. I want to restore the Castle to what it was originally. My grandfather sold a lot of our pictures. One day I hope to buy them back."

"Can you not do it now?" Virginia asked.

A sudden darkness seemed to cloud his face.

"I am afraid I cannot afford it," he said.

It seemed to her that a dozen questions trembled on her lips and she almost asked them in spite of herself. She longed to ask him what he had done with the two million dollars he had received on his marriage to her; what he was doing with her fortune which, undoubtedly, he must be drawing on month after month. So much money and yet he could not afford a few pictures.

The Duke closed the window almost as if he deliberately shut out the vista to punish himself—or her.

"Well, Miss Langholme," he said in a very different tone, "I hope you find everything you want. If not, ask Matthews—he is the butler. My own secretary is on holiday at the moment but, doubtless, Miss Marshbanks will look after you. And, now, if you will excuse me."

"Of course," Virginia said. "And thank you very much for showing me round."

The Duke turned and left her and went from the library shutting the door behind him. When he had gone Virginia sat down in one of the red, leather-covered chairs and tried to think.

All through the conversation she had felt as if the strangeness and embarrassment of it would strangle her voice within her throat, and yet somehow she had come through it. What was all this talk of money? And for the first time since she had left the *boudoir* she could feel astonished at the Duchess's behaviour. Grateful for five pounds! What could it mean? And those men who had come to see her jewellery! What was happening at the Castle? And why, indeed, were they so poor? It seemed an unfathomable mystery; for she realised it was something about which she could not make inquiries, not even of Miss Marshbanks.

"All the same, I shall find out," she promised herself, and then found it hard to go on worrying when she looked around the library.

Because she could not resist it, she climbed up the small, twisting staircase to the gallery and there she discovered were some of the smaller and perhaps rarer books. Many of them looked incredibly old. She moved along the gallery touching first one and then another, and found at the end of it, directly over the fireplace, there were two little alcoves with red leather seats and high, scholars' desks at which one could sit and read.

Like a child with a new toy she seated herself in one of the alcoves, and as she did so she heard the door into the library below open and someone come in. She realised she was out of sight and because for a moment she could not steel herself to face the Duke again, she kept still. He would think she had gone, she thought, and not be surprised at her absence.

A moment later, as she had anticipated, she heard the door reopen and then, to her surprise, there came a voice:

"Hello, Marcus! What are you doing here?"

It was a woman who spoke and she drawled her words in a manner which was fascinating and rather attractive.

"Shelmadine! I thought you were with Sebastian."

"He escaped me," came the reply. "I think he went up to see his mother."

"And how are you progressing?" the man asked.

"Not very well," the woman who was called Shelmadine replied. "He is charming but we get no further. Do you think he can still be wearing his heart out for Millicent?"

"Good gracious, no!" the man replied. "Not after she treated him so badly. He was broken-hearted at the time, of course, who would not be? Millicent broke more hearts than any other woman has ever managed to do. But you forget, Sebastian has been married since then."

"I forget nothing," Shelmadine said. "She is in a lunatic asylum or something, so we need not count her."

The man gave a laugh.

"Fortunate for me, was it not? I should have been really out of the race if she had produced an heir."

"My dear Marcus! Sebastian is a young man. You are very, very much an outsider."

The drawling voice ceased suddenly and then Shelmadine said:

"Oh, my dear! Do not make me love you too much. It makes my part all the more difficult for me."

"Shelmadine!" The man's voice was hoarse. Then there was silence and Virginia realised they must be in each other's arms. She wondered wildly whether she ought to declare her presence and then decided it would be far too embarrassing.

"Damn you, Shelmadine! You go to a man's head!" the man called Marcus ejaculated after a long pause.

"Oh, Marcus, we have got to be together!" Shelmadine cried passionately. "We have got to! We cannot go on like this. My dressmaker threatens to sue me if I have not paid at least half my bill by the end of the week."

"Do not talk to me of bills," Marcus said. "The places I can go in London are getting few and far between, I can tell you."

"We must do something," Shelmadine said despairingly.

"You have another go at him tonight," Marcus said, "take him out in the moonlight or something. What about going to his bedroom?"

"It is too obvious," Shelmadine protested. "I do not believe he would fall for that sort of thing. What is the matter with him? He has had enough mistresses in the past. What about that Gaiety girl you told me about?"

"I know! I know!" Marcus said. "But since the old man died he seems to have become quite different. And he is certainly not very helpful where I am concerned. God! How I hate him! He stands between me and everything that matters."

"Dearest, I must go."

"Yes, of course. We must not be found here together. It is about the only place no one comes. Those old cronies are always peeping and peering about the place."

"Ghastly old creatures," Shelmadine shuddered. "The only thing they are interested in is money."

Marcus laughed bitterly. "Aren't we all?"

"But we are different," Shelmadine said. "I do not want to gamble all night. I just want to live so that I do not tremble at every knock at the door and feel afraid to open each letter that comes for me."

"If you feel like that," Marcus said, "think of me. Blast it, Shelmadine! I wish to God he were dead!"

There was a moment's silence and then Virginia heard Shelmadine say:

"Goodbye!" There was the sound of the door opening and shutting.

She waited some minutes before she heard whoever had been left leave the room. She then realised that she had been almost holding her breath for fear she would be discovered.

Who were they? And what did the conversation mean? Was everybody in the Castle besotted with the idea of money? And why did Marcus, whoever he might be, hate the Duke, and wish him dead? It seemed an insoluble mystery and she felt overpowered by it all. She had a sudden desire to return to America. She had seen all she had come to see and now she longed to go away.

Slowly she climbed down the staircase to the floor of the library. She felt almost as if she had dreamed the conversation she had heard without seeing the people concerned. She felt, too, that all she had heard in the Duchess' *boudoir* was quite unreal.

She opened the library door and walked down the passage to the great hall. As she got there she saw that a woman was crossing the marble floor and ascending the staircase. She was very elegantly dressed in an afternoon gown of blue satin trimmed with lace frills and there was a big, red rose at her breast. Her hair was raven black.

"She was beautiful," Virginia thought as she watched her walking up the staircase with an elegance that was artificial and yet, in itself, very graceful. She had nearly reached the landing and Virginia was just about to move down the passage when the Duke came out into the hall

"Lady Shelmadine!" he called. "You are not leaving us? There is something I particularly wanted to show you."

She turned and looked down at him over the banisters, her face very lovely in the evening light coming through the long windows. Her skin was magnolia, her eyebrows were winged over eyes which were surprisingly green.

"I think you have missed your opportunity," she said. "You have neglected me for so long, I am going to my room to lie down."

"Forgive me," he pleaded, "and come down again. We need you."

"Are you really sorry?" she pouted.

"Truly penitent," he replied gaily.

"Very well. On this occasion I will forgive you," she said. "But you have been very neglectful of me the whole afternoon."

"Then I must apologise," the Duke said. "But come now, the others are waiting."

She came down on to the last step but one of the stairs and held out her hands.

"Say you are sorry," she commanded him, and he bent and kissed her fingers. "You have been very unkind," she said in a low, seductive voice.

"I have not meant to be," he answered. "But I had urgent matters which required my attention."

"Nothing should be more urgent than us."

She looked into his eyes and there was no mistaking her meaning. The Duke merely laughed.

"You cannot go on rebuking me," he said. "I am forgiven!"

She stepped into the hall and slipped her arm through

his, and they passed together through a doorway and out of sight.

Virginia stood very still. No one had noticed her in the shadows at the end of the passage. Then, feeling suddenly insignificant and very much alone, she climbed the staircase towards her bedroom.

5

"THE Duchess liked you! And I can assure you, Miss Langholme, Her Grace is difficult to please," Miss Marshbanks said to Virginia as they finished dinner in their small sitting-room.

They had been waited on by a footman and all the dishes had been served on crested silver. There were candles on the table and Virginia could not help feeling that had she been with anyone but Miss Marshbanks it would have been a romantic setting.

Miss Marshbanks certainly kept up appearances. She was wearing an evening dress, very elaborate and be-frilled, of rusty black net, and she had changed her ordinary, every-day pince-nez for gold ones hung from a gold chain set with garnets. She wore a garnet bracelet and garnet earrings dangling from her ears twinkled in the candlelight.

"How nice of Her Grace," Virginia said with what she hoped was befitting humility.

"I assure you it is a compliment for Her Grace to take to anyone new," Miss Marshbanks said with the air of a school-mistress bestowing a special prize on a favoured pupil. "They are all very conventional here at the Castle and a new face is not *persona grata*—if you know what I mean."

"Surely a lot of new faces must come here," Virginia suggested. "Have you not got a party staying in the Castle at the moment?"

"Oh, no, not a party!" Miss Marshbanks appeared quite shocked. "It is only just eight months since the late Duke died—such a nice man and always most gracious to me—and so Her Grace is still in mourning. However, as you realise, she can wear mauve and grey, but entertaining is definitely not possible for another four months."

"But I thought I saw some guests," Virginia persisted.

"Not guests—friends," Miss Marshbank corrected. "Let

me see, there are not more than ten people staying at the moment."

"And that is not a party I suppose!" Virginia exclaimed.

"Indeed, not!" Miss Marshbanks replied with a silvery laugh. "Not when we are used to crowds, as you might say. At the moment there are only Her Grace's special friends like Colonel Cholmondeley, Sir David Wenthorn and Lord Crawford. Of course, poor Lord Rufton is in the house but then he hardly counts."

Virginia wanted to ask why not but it was not possible to stop Miss Marshbanks.

"Then there is Lady Shelmadine Dutton," she added and her voice seemed to sharpen.

"Who is she?" Virginia managed to interpose.

"I am really not interested in Lady Shelmadine," Miss Marshbanks said primly.

"But do tell me about her," Virginia insisted.

"She is not a person whom I care to discuss," Miss Marshbanks said. "It surprises me that His Grace encourages her to come here. As I said to the Duchess only last week, it is not as if she is a relation or even a very old friend. Of course, His Grace did know her husband."

"She is married!" Virginia ejaculated.

"A widow," Miss Marshbanks replied. "Her husband was killed in the Boer War. He was at Oxford with the Duke. But I do not believe His Grace had ever met Lady Shelmadine until she almost forced herself upon him."

Miss Marshbanks put down her coffee cup and leaned across the table. The footman had left the room and they were quite alone.

"I do not mind telling you, Miss Langholme, that I have my suspicions about Lady Shelmadine. I have an idea that she is chasing the Duke! Of course he is married but that will not stop her trying to capture him."

"Do you really think so?" Virginia asked in an appropriate tone of astonishment and trying not to laugh. She had a sudden vision of the Duke being roped like a steer.

"She is brazen! That's what I think," Miss Marshbanks exploded. "Brazen in the way she carries on. All those low-cut dresses and the manner in which she sidles up to a man, flashing her eyelashes. She has no use for women, I can tell you that! And not the right attitude toward the servants. Why, Ellen—she is the head housemaid—was telling me Lady Shelmadine was quite sharp because she thought one of her dresses had not been pressed properly. And the tips she gives are hardly worth having."

"Perhaps Lady Shelmadine has no money," Virginia suggested.

"If she is so poverty stricken, then she should not be staying in places like this," Miss Marshbanks said severely. "We have a certain standard to keep up at Ryll and at the moment I consider it most unseemly that Lady Shelmadine should be continually inviting herself to stay. Not that the Duke does not aid and abet her; but, then, what can you expect of men?"

"Do you think that the Duke is interested in Lady Shelmadine?" Virginia asked, choosing her words.

"No, I do not," Miss Marshbanks replied. "I do not think he is interested in anybody except himself. If ever there was a selfish man it is His Grace. But, then, as I have said, all men are selfish; I have no use for any of them. When I think of Her Grace, so lonely and pathetic, and her own son so harsh to her, it makes my blood boil, it does really."

"What does His Grace do that is so harsh?" Virginia inquired.

Miss Marshbanks seemed to draw back with a sudden snap.

"What must you think of me," she asked affectedly, "gossiping away about my employers to a stranger! You must not ask me too much, you must not really. You see, I have a very special place in this household. I am much more than a secretary to the Duchess. In fact," Miss Marshbanks simpered a little, "I am more like a lady-in-waiting. As a matter of fact, the dear King, when he was Prince of Wales, actually suggested that. 'Is this your lady-in-waiting?' he asked Her Grace when I brought to her a purse which she had forgotten. How we laughed about it afterwards! She often refers to me as her 'lady-in-waiting', and I am afraid I sometimes think of myself in that capacity."

"Being an American I do not know what a lady-in-waiting does," Virginia said, "but I am sure you make a very good one."

"Although I should not say it, I do," Miss Marshbanks replied. "There is nothing that goes on in this house that I do not know about. In that way I try to shield Her Grace from worries and upsets. She is frail and not as young as she used to be. I cannot make the Duke understand that to keep her happy he should allow her to do more or less what she wants."

"And can she not?" Virginia asked.

Again that look of secretiveness came over Miss Marshbanks' face.

"What woman can?" she asked evasively. "I do not mind telling *you*, Miss Langholme, a very big secret—but, of course, I trust you not to relate it to anyone."

"Naturally, I will not repeat anything you tell me in confidence," Virginia said. Miss Marshbanks leaned across the table again.

"Very well," she said. "I am a Socialist!"

"A Socialist!" Virginia exclaimed. "But I thought they were against the rich!"

"That is what I am," Miss Marshbanks said. "The only exception being Her Grace. If I told you a quarter of what I have seen in this Castle I would make your hair stand on end! In fact I am against the aristocracy and all that they stand for."

Virginia repressed a smile. She could not help thinking that Miss Marshbanks would be very lost and unhappy outside the aristocratic atmosphere in which she obviously revelled.

"You will not mention this to Her Grace, will you?" Miss Marshbanks asked. "It would upset her if she thought I had such ideas; but, there, I was always a rebel."

Again Virginia smiled, and then because she was curious she tried to get back to the subject of Lady Shelmadine.

"I saw a very attractive lady as I was coming through the hall this evening," she said. "Perhaps it was the person of whom you were speaking. She was very elegantly dressed and had dark hair and a very white skin."

"That is Lady Shelmadine," Miss Marshbanks said. "I think, myself, she sometimes looks like a witch! I would not put it past her to cast some evil spells if she thought she would gain by them."

"There was somebody else with her," Virginia went on, "and I thought she called him Marcus."

"Oh, that is Captain Marcus Ryll," Miss Marshbanks explained. "A charming young man. He is the heir presumptive, of course!"

"The heir to what?" Virginia inquired.

"The Dukedom," Miss Marshbanks said. "His father was the younger brother of the last Duke and if anything happens to His Grace and he dies without having children—which for reasons I won't mention seems likely—then Captain Marcus will inherit."

"In which case, should he not have a title or something?" Virginia inquired.

Miss Marshbanks shook her head.

"No, indeed! The younger sons of Dukes have a courtesy title of Lord, but their sons have no distinctive rank."

"I could never remember all those things!" Virginia exclaimed.

"We have a book which lists them all," Miss Marshbanks said, "so it is not so difficult. And, of course, when one is constantly with such people one gets used to knowing what is right and what is wrong."

"Of course," Virginia murmured.

"I must say, I like Captain Marcus," Miss Marshbanks said dreamily. "He is always one for a joke, and is invariably hail-fellow-well-met and not given to black moods like some people we could name!"

"Do you mean the Duke?" Virginia asked.

"You never know what mood His Grace will be in," Miss Marshbanks replied, her voice dropping again. "Two days ago I passed him on the stairs and I promise you as truly as I am sitting here he never even saw me. Of course, he had been with Her Grace, upsetting her again—bullying her is what I call it—and leaving her almost in tears. I should like to give His Grace a piece of my mind, but what good would it do? He does not care what people say or think, he just goes his own way and it is his mother who suffers most."

"Must she live with him if they are so unhappy together?" Virginia said. "Has she no money of her own?"

"I cannot discuss it, Miss Langholme," Miss Marshbanks replied. "I know a great deal of secret information which must not pass my lips. But I can tell you one thing: Her Grace offered to go and live in the Dower House. She said to me at the time: "Marshy, I think we would be very happy there, you and I. We would have people we wanted to stay and a lot of fun on our own." But the Duke would not hear of it. No, he insisted on her staying at the Castle. I thought it was just downright selfishness myself."

"It does seem like it," Virginia said slowly. "But what would happen if the Duke's wife came to live here?"

Virginia could not resist asking the question.

"Oh, then I imagine Her Grace would leave," Miss Marshbanks replied. "But there seems no likelihood of that happening, from all accounts the new Duchess has never gained consciousness since the wedding."

"Does anyone mind—her . . . her being so ill?" Virginia asked.

Miss Marshbanks hesitated then answered:

"It's a bit of a mystery, Miss Langholme! Most unexpectedly His Grace went to America—of course, he had not inherited the Dukedom then because his father was alive—and the next thing we learned was that he was married! The newspapers were full of it! Apparently his bride collapsed immediately after the ceremony!"

"And when he returned?" Virginia prompted. She knew she should not be so curious but she longed to know what they had thought of that horrible wedding in England.

"Do you know," Miss Marshbanks said, lowering her voice, "she is never mentioned. There was at the time a terrible row between His Grace and his mother, then silence! I have often tried to make Her Grace speak of her daughter-in-law, but she refuses. I feel in my bones that something very strange happened, Miss Langholme, but it remains a mystery—just a mystery."

"Perhaps one day you will learn the truth," Virginia said.

"I am sure I shall," Miss Marshbanks replied confidently, "and if there was trouble I know who was to blame. Men are all the same and I shall be very surprised if you leave the Castle without feeling that the best thing for all women would be for them to fight for Women's Suffrage. If I were not so busy I would go and join the organisation in London, that is what I would do."

"I am sure Her Grace would not like that," Virginia said with a smile.

"No, indeed, she would be lost without me. But one day I will unfurl the flag for women's rights," Miss Marshbanks asserted, "and then we will see if the men can go on bossing us about."

She turned and, looking at the clock over the mantelpiece, rose to her feet.

"I must just slip upstairs and take Her Grace's pug for a walk," she said. "The poor old dog is very rheumaticky and those young footmen hurry him along too fast. As Her Grace has often said to me: "There is no one with whom I can trust poor Dizzy—he is named after Disraeli, one of our famous Prime Ministers—except you, Marshy!" So every night about this time I take him for walkies. I shall not be long."

Miss Marshbanks went from the room and Virginia leaned back in her chair and smiled. She was fascinated by Miss Marshbanks' flow of gossip, but she was finding that the information she received was leaving her more and more bewildered.

Why did the Duke bully his mother and what was the explanation for his behaviour? Then there were the jewellers who had called to see the Duchess. Why were they barred the house? And the thing which had apparently escaped the eagle eye of Miss Marshbanks or her informants was that Lady Shelmadine, even if she were chasing the Duke as Miss Marshbanks suspected, was very involved with Captain Marcus Ryll.

At the moment, Virginia told herself, it was rather like a mad jig-saw puzzle. None of the pieces seemed to fit and yet she felt that somewhere there was a clue to it all. She had a sudden desire for air. There was something about the Castle which made her feel overpowered and that already she was becoming embroiled in the intrigues and secrets of the vast and ancient pile.

When she changed for dinner into a simple dress of pale green chiffon, Virginia had brought downstairs a wrap which went with it. Now she picked it up off the chair and going from the sitting-room found her way back to the Great Hall. There was no one about, so she opened the front door herself and went down the stone steps. She crossed the drive and wended her way over the soft grass towards the lake.

It was a very warm evening without a breath of wind; the sun was sinking in a blaze of glory behind the distant woods. It was still light but already, high in the sky, was the first twinkle of an evening star. Virginia reached the lake. The swans were moving over its smooth surface; the island in the centre was a blaze of roses and the little white temple that she had seen from the windows of the Castle was, from here, almost hidden by flowering honeysuckle and silvery white birch trees.

She walked round the lake to where the path led her into a small shrubbery. Birds were nesting in the trees and rabbits scuttled across the path and into the bushes as she approached. It was so peaceful that she felt that all the anxieties which had beset her since she had arrived in

England, and her fear of coming to the Castle, seemed to vanish.

There was a seat in an arbour surrounded by trees and shrubs, with a grass walk in front of it leading down to a lovely statue of a dancing faun. She sat down on the seat and wished that Aunt Ella May was with her to enjoy this moment of peace. This was the real England, she thought. There was something warm and secure about it after all. She felt as if the creatures of the woods, the very air itself, were trying to tell her not to be afraid, to enjoy what they had to offer and to stop running away from reality. "It is all so complicated," she said aloud.

"What is?" a voice asked, startling her and making her jump, so that instinctively her hands went up to quell the tumult in her breast.

Standing on the path opposite to the way by which she had approached the arbour was the Duke. He was wearing evening dress and his white shirt-front gleamed vividly against the darkness of the trees.

"I thought for a moment you were the White Lady," he said with a smile. "I was quite relieved to hear you speak."

"The White Lady?" Virginia questioned.

"She is the family ghost," he replied. "But she only appears when a member of the family is going to die."

"Well, I am glad I am not the bearer of bad news," Virginia smiled.

He came forward and sat beside her on the seat.

"How did you find your way here? Very few people ever visit this little glade."

"Is it private property?" Virginia asked.

"Not where you are concerned," he replied. "But as a general rule I am its only visitor."

"I just seemed to arrive here by chance," Virginia said. "I came for a walk because . . ." She stopped, feeling it would be rude to say she wished to escape from the Castle.

"I know why you came," the Duke said quietly. "You felt that the Castle was too overpowering and for the moment you wanted to escape from it."

"How did you know?" Virginia asked, in some surprise.

"Shall I say I read your thoughts?" the Duke said.

"I supposed all very big houses make one feel small and insignificant," Virginia said.

"I hope my home will not make you feel like that, not for long at any rate," the Duke replied. "I should like you to enjoy yourself here."

"That is very gracious of you," Virginia answered conventionally.

"I sounded patronising," the Duke apologised, "and I did not mean to be. I just wanted an American to see England at its best. And to my mind Ryll Castle is one of the most beautiful places in England."

"It is beautiful indeed," Virginia said quietly.

"It is funny, you know," the Duke went on, looking not at her but down the glade towards the statue, "but I find you easy to talk to—unlike most of the Americans I meet."

"Have you met many?" Virginia inquired.

He shook his head.

"No, I have been only once in America for a very short time. But they gave me the feeling that I had nothing in common with them or they with me. I dare say it is very stupid; they are all people. But with you it seems different."

"I am one hundred per cent American," Virginia said positively.

"And a very attractive one, if I may say so," the Duke said.

She felt herself stiffen at the compliment. She had the feeling that had she been an English girl in the same circumstances he would not have spoken quite like that.

"Tell me about your work," the Duke said, "and about your country."

"Why do you not go to America again and find out about it yourself?" Virginia asked.

It seemed to her that a shadow passed over his face.

"Perhaps one day I will," he said. "At the moment I have an enormous amount of work to do here."

"Work?" she asked with a little smile.

"I see," he said, "that you think that anyone who is not actually earning money is not working. That, if I may say so, is a very American idea of something which is quite unrelated to fact. I work very much harder than my agent whom I pay. I work very much harder than the steward of my household, whom I also pay. What is more, I take the full responsibility not only for what I do but for what they do. Would you not call that work?"

"I suppose I do not understand what people do in a position like yours," Virginia explained. "All the men I have ever known who had money always worked in an office; or they travelled round inspecting branches of their

74

business; they had a dozen secretaries, managers, employees all carrying out their commands."

"Yes, that is big business," the Duke said. "But here at Ryll we are like a small independent country—a state within a state, you might say. I employ nearly a thousand people one way or another. There are not only the household staff but all the other departments—the stonemasons, the carpenters, the laundry; we even have our own brewery. I should like to show you all these things. I think you would realise that in my own way I am quite a business manager."

"I should very much like to see them," Virginia said.

"Then that is a bargain," the Duke smiled. "I will show you England and you will tell me about America."

He held out his hand and she put hers into it. She felt the strength of his fingers and then he looked down at her hand almost reflectively before he let it go. She had a fleeting impression that he hesitated whether he should kiss it, and then she told herself that it was an absurd idea. Yet, feeling a little embarrassed, she rose to her feet.

"I think it is time I went back to the Castle," she said. "Miss Marshbanks will be wondering what has happened to me."

"Is that woman looking after you properly?" the Duke demanded. "I wish it were someone else."

"But, why?" Virginia asked. "Miss Marshbanks has been most kind."

"She has been with us a long time," he said, "and my mother is fond of her." He seemed about to say something else then changed his mind.

They strolled back through the shrubs at the edge of the lake.

"Did you really come from America all by yourself?" the Duke asked.

The last dying rays of the sun were on Virginia's hair.

"Oh, I had a chaperon," Virginia answered. "She retired to her cabin the moment we left New York and did not get up again until we sighted Southampton."

"Then I suppose you had a very amusing time," the Duke said. "Unless, of course, the men on the ship were segregated from the female of the species."

"I do not think I spoke to anyone," Virginia answered. "I had a lot to think about."

"I cannot imagine an English girl travelling alone

without getting into all sorts of trouble," the Duke said. "I admire the independence of your country-women."

"There did not seem to me any danger of getting into any sort of trouble," Virginia said rather coldly.

"I stand corrected," the Duke replied. "All the same, I think you are a brave young woman and I admire you for it."

"I must go back to the Castle," Virginia said again.

"If I walk back with you it will give Miss Marshbanks far too much to gossip about," the Duke said, "so I shall let you go alone. But I have a suggestion to make. Do you ride?"

"Yes, of course," Virginia answered. "I have not, as a matter of fact, ridden for the past three years, but I used to ride a great deal."

"Then ride with me early tomorrow morning," the Duke suggested. "The estate is worth seeing before the world is, what my Nanny used to call, 'well aired'."

"What do you call early?" Virginia inquired.

"Six o'clock at the front door," he said. "There will be nobody else about, I warn you."

"I should like to come," Virginia answered, "and I shall not keep you waiting."

"I shall look forward to it," the Duke said. "Good night, Miss Langholme!"

"Good night!" Virginia answered.

She turned and walked away from him up towards the Castle. The lights were now gleaming in the windows and it looked very vast and very imposing. She knew the Duke was watching her but she forced herself not to look back. She felt as she walked away that she was in some way taking a momentous step which she could not understand and which, for the moment, made no sense.

He had asked her to go riding. She felt a little tingle of pleasure at the idea—and then, suddenly, she knew that in some subtle way it was an insult. She realised that he would never have thought of inviting an unmarried English girl to accompany him unchaperoned, to meet him almost clandestinely so early in the morning. And she knew it was not only because she was an American but also because from a social point of view she had no standing. She was a librarian, someone who ate with Miss Marshbanks, someone with whom the Duke might talk or flirt but with whom such a relationship would have no real significance for him.

The realisation swept over her to leave her, for the moment, almost breathless with anger. And then, almost despite herself, she began to laugh. She could not help seeing the humour of it, knowing that if she were not treated as a Duchess it was entirely her own fault.

She would have liked to go straight to her bedroom, but because she thought it would be rude to Miss Marshbanks, she turned towards the sitting-room. Just as she was leaving the hall a man came out of one of the doors and she almost bumped into him.

"I am sorry," she apologised, and guessed, although she had never seen him, that it was Captain Marcus Ryll.

"Good evening!" he said in puzzled tones. "I do not think we have met before."

"No," Virginia answered.

"I am Marcus Ryll. Are you staying in the Castle?" he asked, noting her evening dress and the fact that her head was uncovered.

"I arrived today," Virginia replied, "from America. I have permission to study some of the books in the library."

"By Jove! How interesting!" Captain Ryll exclaimed.

He took an eye-glass from a waistcoat pocket and set it in his eye. There was something about the very high, white collar he affected, the padded shoulders of his evening coat, the carnation in his buttonhole, the twisted ends of his small moustache, which told Virginia he was exactly what she had seen in caricatures of the English.

"I know!" she exclaimed impulsively, "you are what they call a 'toff', or is it a 'masher'?"

Captain Ryll threw back his head.

"You are right," he laughed. "Bull's eye first time! Where did you hear of such things?"

"Even in the backwoods we sometimes hear of other countries," Virginia answered.

"I apologise," he said. "But you and I must get together. You are far too pretty to spend your time poring over all those dusty books."

"It is what I am here to do," Virginia said.

"That is nonsense!" he retorted. "I will take you out driving. You would like that, would you not?"

"It is very kind of you," Virginia answered, "but I doubt if I shall have the time."

She tried to move away from him down the passage but he barred her way.

"Do you know, you are the prettiest creature I have seen

for years!" he said. "I did not know America could produce anything like you."

"I think, Captain Ryll, that I must find Miss Marshbanks," Virginia said coldly.

"Do not worry about old Marshy. She is not going to monopolise you," he said. "Come out with me and have a look at the moonlight."

He offered her his arm but Virginia managed to slip past him. As he reached out to catch hold of her she was already hurrying down the passage.

"Good night, Captain Ryll!" she called over her shoulder.

"Here, do not go! Stay and have a chat," he cried, but already she had reached the sanctuary of the sitting-room and shut the door behind her.

She was laughing, but at the same time she was annoyed by his impertinence. How dare he treat her in such a cheap, familiar manner? And yet whom had she to blame but Aunt Ella May, who had thought out this apparently very vulnerable disguise?

The sitting-room was empty. Miss Marshbanks, it seemed, was still occupied in walking Dizzy or else she had gone to bed, so Virginia felt she must find her way upstairs and somehow avoid encountering the over-eager attentions of Captain Marcus Ryll.

She peeped out of the door. There was no one about and she decided that there must be another staircase by which she could reach the top landing. Accordingly, instead of turning right she turned left and after a time found the staircase she was seeking. It led her up to the next floor and, a little lost and bewildered, she was looking for her room when she heard the Duchess's voice.

"Are you quite sure it has not come?"

"Absolutely sure, Your Grace."

It was Miss Marshbanks who answered.

"But it is nearly a month overdue and His Lordship is beginning to worry about it. I cannot have him worried, you know that, Marshy."

"Yes, indeed, Your Grace."

"There should be another letter on the first of the month, but if this one is late the other might be late too. What do you think can have happened?"

"I cannot think, Your Grace. I have asked everyone and Masters says that nothing has arrived this last fortnight. Of course, he cannot be sure if anything came before that because he was not looking for it then."

"If it had come he would have handled it, would he not?" the Duchess asked.

"Yes, Your Grace."

"I do not know what to do, I really do not, Marshy!"

"Perhaps His Grace . . . ?"

"No, of course I am not going to ask him," the Duchess interposed quickly. "Now, you quite understand, Marshy? Not a word of this must reach His Grace's ears. And you told Masters not to mention it, too, did you not?"

"Yes, Your Grace, but I was only suggesting . . ."

"I have told you, Marshy, you are to mention it to no one—and that is an order."

Virginia realised that she was standing indecisively in the passage, not knowing whether to go forward or back. Then she heard the sound of someone moving away and, rounding the corner, she saw the Duchess receding down the passage, her dress of mauve chiffon billowing out over the carpet. Miss Marshbanks was standing in the door of her bedroom, an unhappy expression on her face.

"Oh, there you are, Miss Langholme!" she exclaimed as she saw Virginia. "I was wondering where on earth you had got to."

"I went for a little walk," Virginia replied. "I am afraid it took longer than I intended."

"Well, I expect you are ready for bed," Miss Marshbanks said.

"Yes, of course. My bedroom is next door, is it not?"

"Two doors to the left," Miss Marshbanks corrected.

"Oh, thank you," Virginia said. "I am afraid I got a little lost."

"Good night, Miss Langholme! I hope you sleep well," Miss Marshbanks said.

Virginia found her own room with a sigh of relief. She felt suddenly very tired. It had been a long day. At the same time, she thought, almost with a sense of irritation, here was yet another unanswered question. What was the letter the Duchess had not received? And why should the Duke not know about it?

She supposed that really there was a perfectly simple answer, to all the problems she had encountered in the last twenty-four hours, and yet, for the moment, the whole thing seemed complicated beyond belief.

She got into bed and shut her eyes, but she found herself going over all the events that had happened since she had first arrived. In particular she could hear the Duke saying, "That is a bargain", taking her hand in his and looking down at it.

She had a feeling that when they had been together that evening he had not looked so cynical or so arrogant. Then she told herself she was only imagining that; he was a man who bullied his mother, who was given to bad temper and black moods and who, as she knew only too well, was a fortune-hunter of the very worst description.

She disliked him—indeed, she hated him! And if Lady Shelmadine was, indeed, a witch they would be well paired together. Resolutely Virginia turned on the pillow. She was not going to think about either of them any more. They were neither of them worth it.

6

VIRGINIA came down the staircase as the big grandfather clock in the hall chimed six o'clock. The Duke had said no one would be about, but he had not, of course, considered the domestic staff as worth a thought.

There were half a dozen bright-cheeked maidservants in print dresses, mob caps and starched aprons, polishing the fire-guards, dusting the furniture, scrubbing the marble hall, brushing the carpets. Footmen, in their shirt-sleeves and striped waistcoats were carrying dirty glasses from the drawing-room, while other servants, lower in the hierarchy, carried in wood and coal and removed the ashes from last night's fires.

The maidservants were all too well trained to stare, but Virginia knew they peeped at her as she passed through the hall and on to the front porch.

The Duke was already astride a magnificent black stallion while a groom held a chestnut mare.

"Good morning!" Virginia said, and knew, although he was too polite to show his surprise, that her appearance was unconventional.

"You must take a riding-habit with you to England," Aunt Ella May had said in New York. "Everyone rides in England. I used to envy them going off on their fine horses while I was left behind with old Mr. Vanderbilt."

"I have not ridden for three years or more," Virginia had objected. "Not since I grew so fat."

"Once you have ridden as well as you used to do," her aunt assured her, "you never forget it. But you must have something in which to ride."

"Then I will wear the sort of clothes I used to wear when we went to Papa's ranch in Texas," Virginia said.

Her aunt had protested but Virginia had insisted on buying a long Mexican divided skirt with a fringed hem, and a sleeveless leather coat with fringed pockets. The colour she had chosen was dark green and with it she wore a long-sleeved blouse of pale yellow silk.

She knew when she glanced at herself in the mirror that she looked lovely, but very unlike an English miss going out to ride with her host. She thought, with a little laugh, of the pictures she had seen of women wearing skin-fitting habits with their skirts draped over a pommel and high, polished top-hats with a veil over the face.

She was hatless but she had pinned up her hair tightly, and it framed her small, eager face as she greeted the Duke.

"Do you intend to ride astride?" he asked.

She knew there was a note of astonishment in his voice.

"It is the way I have always ridden," she replied.

"Very well," he said and, turning to the groom: "A saddle without a pommel—quickly!"

The horse was trotted back to the stables and, in a surprisingly short time, returned with what Virginia knew was a gentleman's saddle on its back. There was a mounting-block beside the front door. She mounted, taking up the reins with experienced hands, and felt a little thrill of delight at feeling the horse, fresh and eager, beneath her.

They moved off without a word and only when they were some way from the great Castle did the Duke say:

"You have obviously ridden a great deal before."

She turned a smiling face towards him.

"Are you shocked at my attire?" she inquired.

"Not shocked," he replied, "only full of admiration. But I dare say in the hunting field it would come in for a lot of criticism."

"I shall have left long before you start hunting," she said.

"I am sorry about that," he replied. "And now let your mare show her paces."

They started off at an easy gallop. Then some mischief

entered into Virginia and she found herself urging her horse on, trying to take the lead, striving to beat the Duke at what she knew was indisputably his best sport.

Now they were galloping neck to neck, tearing over the turf, the only noise the sound of the horses' hooves. Virginia could feel her breath coming quickly between her lips. She felt a strange, almost uncontrollable excitement. She would beat him! She would! And then she knew it was impossible. She rode well but he seemed a part of his own horse, and as suddenly as the race had begun it ended, as they pulled their horses in and stared at each other, breathless, yet at the same time elated as if they had each won a victory.

"You are magnificent!" the Duke exclaimed, and Virginia wondered if she could have heard aright; for as he spoke he turned away towards some trees.

She followed and they twisted and turned until they came upon a narrow path leading, apparently, into the centre of the wood. It was quite a steep ascent and when they reached the top Virginia was astonished to see a house in front of them. It was not very large but beautifully proportioned with a white-pillared entrance. The path broadened and she was able now to ride alongside the Duke.

"Who lives here?" she asked.

"It is mine," he answered. "I want to show it to you and we can also have breakfast."

As he spoke an old man came running round the side of the house to take their horses.

"Good morning, Bates!" the Duke said.

"Good morning, Your Grace! 'Tis a long time since we've seen you. The missus was wondering when you'd pay us a visit."

"Well, I hope you have a good breakfast ready for us," the Duke said.

He swung himself out of the saddle and turned to help Virginia, but she was too quick for him—she sprang lightly to the ground, stopping to pat her horse's neck before she followed the Duke towards the front door.

Already there was someone ready to open it—another old man, dressed in the correct morning-coat of a butler and bowing at the Duke's approach.

"Good morning, Masters!" the Duke said. "Breakfast as soon as possible. We shall be on the terrace."

"Very good, Your Grace."

The house was delightful, exquisitely furnished, with bow windows looking south. They passed through a small salon and the Duke opened a French window on to a paved terrace with a stone balustrade.

Virginia gave a little cry of astonishment, for in front of them lay a magnificent panorama. It was almost as if the house was built on the edge of a small cliff. Below there were green fields and winding streams stretching to a flash of blue on the horizon which she realised was the sea.

"How lovely!" she exclaimed. "And yet you seldom come here."

"I have many houses besides the Castle," the Duke replied, "but this, perhaps, is my favourite. It was built by an ancestor of mine in the eighteenth century and he built it as a secret hiding-place for someone he loved very deeply."

Virginia sat down on the edge of the balustrade. The wind blew the tiny, loose curls of her hair against her forehead.

"Why did not your ancestor, if he was the Duke, marry the lady he loved and take her to the Castle?" she asked.

"She was already married," the Duke explained.

"So it was a clandestine love affair!"

"It was, indeed," the Duke answered. "Her husband was away fighting in America, as it happened. The estates marched with each other but they had to have somewhere to meet."

"So they came here," Virginia said softly.

"They were very happy," the Duke told her. "It is a house of love and he called it 'Queen's Heart' because for him she was a queen."

"What a charming story," Virginia said. "And what happened?"

"Her husband came back from America," the Duke replied. "Perhaps he had learned new ideas in your country! Anyway, he discovered what had been going on, challenged my ancestor to a duel and killed him."

"How terrible!" Virginia cried. "And what happened to the lady?"

"Legend says that he killed her as well. Anyway, it is known that she died a few months after her lover, and it is she who is supposed to haunt the Castle looking for him, especially in the little temple on the lake which is another place where they met. The local people say that she has never found him, and that is why when one of the family dies she is seen looking to see if it is the man she loved coming to her at last. But because of his guilt he is in Hell and so they can never be together again!"

"Oh, no!" Virginia expostulated. "It is too cruel."

"That is what my grandmother used to say," the Duke smiled, "and so she gave it another ending. She said they were together again and so happy that the White Lady comes back to welcome other members of the family so that they can all enjoy the Elysian Fields together."

"I like that ending much better," Virginia said.

"So you are romantic!" the Duke remarked, and she thought there was a little, cynical twist to his lips.

"If you mean by that that I think love between two people is a wonderful thing," Virginia said, "I agree with you. But your ancestor was wrong in what he did and so he paid the price."

"Of course," the Duke answered, "and if I had been the White Lady's husband I should have done exactly the same."

"You would have killed her too?" Virginia asked.

"Perhaps," the Duke replied.

"That is very overbearing and over-possessive," Virginia said. "It would have been more human and sensible to have sought a divorce."

"That is an American point of view," the Duke said. "In England we do not care for scandals in our families and a man must protect his honour the best way he can."

"A cave-man with a club!" Virginia said jeeringly.

"Why not?" the Duke asked. "If a man had a wife, say, as pretty as you, he would need a club, and a very big one, to keep away the thieves and robbers who would envy him his most precious possession."

He was speaking lightly, but there was something in the look of his eyes which made Virginia turn away and she felt a sudden sense of relief when a voice from the house said:

"Breakfast is served, Your Grace!"

The dining-room was octagonal and painted Adam green, with some exquisite Georgian reliefs on the walls picked out in white. There was a sideboard laden with dishes and Virginia stared in amazement at the amount of food which had been procured at such short notice.

"How did they have all this in the house?" she asked.

The Duke smiled as if she were a child asking ridiculous questions.

"Everything is always ready," he said.

"But you might not come here for months!" Virginia protested.

"I do not think I have been here for three, or is it four months, Masters?" he asked the old butler.

"Nearly five, Your Grace. We were beginning to think you had forgotten us."

"And they are always ready?" Virginia asked in awed tones.

"But, of course," the Duke replied. "Just the same as my house in London is ready and my yacht in Southampton can be taken out to sea within a quarter of an hour of my coming aboard."

"It must make you feel very important," she said.

He looked across the table at her and then threw back his head and laughed.

"I cannot think of another woman who would say such a thing to me," he said. "You are refreshingly unique, Miss Langholme. Go on talking to me. I like the sound of your voice with its very faint accent."

"I thought it was you who had the accent," Virginia retorted. "And you must forgive me if I am amused, but everything that happens here in England is so unlike America."

"In what way?" the Duke asked.

"Well, the Castle for one thing," she said. "And the kind of state you keep up everywhere you go."

"Are you still thinking about all these dishes for breakfast?" the Duke asked. "You should see what is laid out at the Castle: half a dozen egg dishes; half a dozen fish; a cold collation of hams, brawns and *pâtés*; and, of course, game in season, grouse, pheasants, snipe; anything a man could fancy with which to start the day."

"It sounds very interesting," Virginia said, "but I am not likely to see it, am I?"

The Duke looked startled.

"I am not complaining," Virginia went on, "do not think that. It is only the conventions and taboos which amuse me. I have been told of how the whole structure of social standing has been evolved down the ages. How the housekeeper and the butler are the most important people below stairs, having their own rooms and being waited on by their own servants, so to speak. And how the housekeeper only talks to your mother's lady's maid as her equal, and that after the servants, male and female, have eaten together in the dining-hall, the maids take up their pudding plates and retire to another room."

"It is fascinating, do go on," the Duke said. "I have forgotten all this myself, although I suppose I knew it once."

"The visiting servants take the precedence of their masters," Virginia continued. "If you have a Princess or a Duchess to stay, her lady's maid goes down to dinner on the arm of the butler, and the same, of course, applies to the housekeeper. And they are addressed by the name of their employer. My maid, if I had one, for instance, would be called 'Miss Langholme'. Poor thing! I fear it would be only the boot-boy, or someone whom I believe is called the knife-boy, who would take her into supper!"

The Duke roared with laughter.

"But you see," Virginia went on, "I have gathered that Miss Marshbanks and I are in a little world of our own, hung, as it were, between heaven and earth. We are the betwixt and betweens. We have no really official positions and therefore I shall never see your great array at breakfast."

Virginia's voice was deliberately wistful.

"You are laughing at me," the Duke said accusingly. "When you are being mischievous there is a little dimple which appears at the side of your mouth. I find it quite irresistible."

Virginia pushed back her chair from the table and walked out on the terrace. She stood for a moment looking out over the view, her back towards the house. She heard him come across to her, his riding-boots heavy on the flagged terrace.

He stood for a moment looking down at her—at her small, straight nose etched against the blue sky, her lips parted, her dark eyes serious and unsmiling.

"Are you angry with me?" he asked in a quiet voice.

"No," she answered quite naturally, "but I am not used to compliments."

"The men in America must all be blind!" he answered. "Do you not realise, Virginia, you are very beautiful? And I want to tell you so."

"It embarrasses me," she said.

"Does it?" he questioned. "You cannot run away from the truth. Sooner or later you will have to listen and if, indeed, I am the first to tell you so, then I count myself very privileged. I love the way your eyes light up when you are excited and go dark, rather troubled, when you do not understand. I love the way your mouth trembles sometimes, as if you were afraid. And your hair—what shall I tell you about your hair, Virginia? Because I have never seen a woman with hair like it. I want . . . I want so much to touch it."

"Stop!"

Virginia turned on him suddenly and stamped her foot.

"You should not say these things to me and I should not listen."

"Why not?" the Duke asked. "What is wrong?"

His question seemed to fall between them like a stone dropped into deep water, and for a moment Virginia knew he had defeated her. She could not tell him why he should not say such things. She could not reply that she knew he was married. She could not put herself in the position of repulsing his supposed advances when, in reality, he had made none.

She could only stand there, nonplussed, feeling herself unaccountably disturbed by his closeness and by what he had said.

"You are so young," the Duke said softly, "so young and so unspoiled. It is a long time, Virginia, since I have been as happy as I am here with you at this moment. Perhaps, after all, this house has a spell cast upon it. Will you come here with me again?"

She turned her head slowly to look at him.

"I wonder if you will ask me," she said. "At the moment I am new, a novelty. But, after all, what can you have in common with an American?"

If she had meant to strike at him she succeeded. She saw his lips tighten and she knew she could read his thoughts and that at that moment he was thinking of another American who bore his name.

"We must go back," he said stiffly.

"Yes, of course," Virginia agreed.

They went through the house. There was the fresh smell of beeswax and flowers, and also, Virginia fancied, there was a feeling of happiness. On an impulse she wanted to say: "Let us stay for a while. Do not let us go back to the Castle but let us linger here, at least for a few hours, so that we can talk to each other."

The Duke had reached the front door and now, as he saw her moving slowly through the hall, he said:

"You like it, do you not? Queen's Heart means something to you."

"I almost feel as if the house is trying to tell me something," Virginia replied.

"I, too, always feel that whenever I come here," the Duke said.

She looked at him in astonishment.

"Why should I pretend?" he said almost roughly, as if she had asked the question. "I love the house and when I am worried or lonely I come to Queen's Heart. Alone!" he added, as if he had guessed that there was another question in her mind.

"Goodbye, Masters!" he said to the old man at the door. "I shall come again soon."

"I hope you will, Your Grace," the butler said. "And the lady, too."

Virginia smiled at him and the other old man brought the horses round from the stables. Virginia looked for a mounting-block, but the Duke lifted her up in his arms and swung her on to the saddle.

"You are as light as the proverbial feather," he said. "It is not fashionable to be so thin, but you make every other woman seem fat and clumsy. When I look at you I feel you are a spirit from the woods, or perhaps I should say from the sea, blown to me, perchance, by a wind from the Atlantic."

She smiled down at him as he stood with his hand on the bridle of her horse.

"You are very poetic," she said teasingly.

"I never knew I was until today," he answered.

They rode back to the Castle almost in silence, and when they reached the stables Virginia dismounted and went straight into the Castle without waiting for the Duke. She had the feeling that he lingered deliberately so they should not be seen entering together.

In her own room she stood for a moment with her hands against her hot cheeks, staring at herself in the glass. Was he just an accomplished flirt? The kind of man who never leaves a pretty woman alone? Or was he, indeed, as he appeared to be, attracted by her? It would be ironic, she thought to herself, if she could make him fall in love with her. And the idea came to her that this, indeed, would be a just punishment. He would love the wife whom he had married entirely for her money and she could denounce him for the fortune-hunter that he was. He would then learn how deeply she despised him.

"He is despicable," she said aloud, but somehow the words did not seem convincing even to her own ears. "Look how he has behaved," she told her conscience. And yet she could think of nothing but how handsome he looked astride the great, black stallion; how she had been forced to turn aside from that look in his eyes because it made her feel shy; and how his words produced an unaccountable tremor within her throat she had never experienced before.

"I should go back to America," she told her reflection in the mirror, and knew that she would not leave.

An hour or so later, dressed demurely in a morning dress of deep blue with white muslin collar and cuffs, she settled down to work in the Library. She took down books from the shelves but all she could find were pictures of the Duke. His ancestors all looked like him; the same straight, aristocratic nose, the broad forehead, the rather square chin and, in some of them, that look of cynical detachment.

Book after book gave her only the history of the Ryll family and nothing else, and she was just putting a heavily tooled, leather-bound history of the Castle back into its place when the door of the library opened. She looked over her shoulder and knew that it was the Duke, and that somehow she had been waiting for him.

"How are you getting on?" he asked, and she had to look away from him because of the expression in his eyes.

"I am finding it difficult to know where to start," she answered.

"I must come and help you," he said. "At the moment I have brought you an old map of the estate. I thought it would amuse you to see where we rode this morning. It was made just after Queen's Heart was built, and my ancestor had further plans which, of course, were never completed because he was killed."

"I should love to see them," Virginia said.

The Duke put the large folder down on the leather-topped desk in the centre of the room.

"I have got a lot more deeds and things in my own study," he said. "I just picked these up at random. If you are interested we can go through them one day."

There was an eagerness in his suggestion. Preventing herself from agreeing enthusiastically to the idea, Virginia forced herself to reply:

"I doubt if I shall have time. There is so much to do before I return to America."

"Why do you keep talking about leaving?" the Duke inquired. "You have only just arrived. History was not made in a day and you cannot write about it in a few weeks nor, indeed, a few months. You know that my mother and I like having you here."

"How can you say that when I have only just arrived?" Virginia asked.

"I do not take long to make up my mind about a person," the Duke said. "From the moment I saw you standing in my mother's room I knew that you were different."

Virginia was silent. She remembered that she had seen him before she had even entered the Castle. In his anger at the men he had thrown out he had not noticed her. The memory of it made her angry.

"I must get back to work, Your Grace," she said coldly. "Thank you for the plans."

"I want to show them to you myself," the Duke said. He opened the folder but at that moment the butler came in the library. "What is it, Matthews?" the Duke asked irritably.

"They have sent from the stables to say that the horses you wished to see, Your Grace, have arrived."

"Well, in that case I must come at once," the Duke replied. "I am sorry, Miss Langholme, but I told a horse-dealer who has some very fine-quality animals for sale that I should like to see them. Will you excuse me?"

"Of course," Virginia answered. She wanted to add that she would like to see the horses, too, but knew that such an idea would seem presumptuous.

"I shall not be long," the Duke said softly, and leaving the folder on the table he went from the library.

Virginia mentally gave herself a little shake and went back to the books, but she had barely glanced at one before the door opened once again and the Duchess came in.

"Good morning, Miss Langholme!"

The Duchess rustled into the room, wearing a magnificent grey gown trimmed with lace. Diamonds sparkled in her ears and a great string of pearls hung down from her neck to her tiny waist. She was holding by the lead her old pug, who was far too fat to move quickly and was snuffling and snorting as he followed her.

"Good morning, Your Grace!" Virginia replied.

"I understood my son was here," the Duchess said, looking round as if to see if the Duke was concealing himself among the bookcases.

"He was a few moments ago," Virginia said, "but he was wanted down at the stables to see some horses."

"Horses! Horses! That is all men think about!" the Duchess exclaimed. "Although, I must say, I enjoy them myself if they are racing. Have you been to any races, Miss Langholme?"

"Only a long time ago in America," Virginia answered.

"It is very exciting," the Duchess said, and now there was a sudden warmth in her voice. "I know of no greater thrill than to see a horse on which one has staked a large amount of money pass the winning-post."

She gave a little sigh and added:

"Of course, it is not so amusing when one has lost!"

"No, I can understand that," Virginia smiled.

The Duchess turned as if she would leave the library and then saw the folder on the table.

"What is this?" she asked.

"I believe it contains some old maps which the Duke was going to show me," Virginia answered.

The Duchess flicked over the cover. Inside the folder, on top of what were obviously the old and mellowed vellums of the maps, were several open letters and on the very top was an envelope.

The Duchess gave a little cry.

"But, that is for Lord Rufton!" she exclaimed. "It is the letter I have been expecting for weeks. How has Sebastian got hold of it?"

She picked it up and turned it over. It had not been opened.

"I cannot understand it, but at least it is here," the Duchess went on. "Oh, I am glad to have found it!"

Virginia felt that she ought to say that the folder belonged to the Duke, and then she told herself it was none of her business.

"I must go to His Lordship at once," the Duchess said. "At once! Where is Miss Marshbanks?"

"She told me at breakfast-time that she was going into the village in the pony-cart," Virginia answered.

"Oh . . . yes, of course!" the Duchess said. "I had a message for the Vicar. She said she would take it. Oh, dear! I shall have to wait for her return . . . that is, unless . . . you would come with me."

"Come with you?" Virginia inquired.

"Yes," the Duchess replied. "To see Lord Rufton. It would be very kind of you if you would."

"But, of course, if you want me," Virginia answered.

"Then come along! Let us go at once," the Duchess said, holding the letter in her hand.

She opened the library door before Virginia could reach it, then going into the hall she handed the pug's lead to a waiting footman.

"Take Dizzy outside, James."

"Very good, Your Grace."

"And now we will go to Lord Rufton," the Duchess said to Virginia.

They started up the staircase.

"You see, Lord Rufton is not very well," the Duchess explained, "and sometimes he is a little . . . troublesome. So my son has made me promise that I will never see him alone. Usually Miss Marshbanks comes with me, but as she is away I really cannot wait for her return. If you are there it will be quite all right."

"What is wrong with him?" Virginia asked.

"I think he is just old," the Duchess said, "and his mind wanders at times. But he is a very, very dear friend. He was a *beau* of mine for years."

She gave a little sigh.

"I should like you to have seen me when I was young. I was so gay and, though I say it, very attractive. They always said I was the most beautiful Duchess in England and, between ourselves, Miss Langholme, it was true! I had a mass of admirers. The girls these days do not seem to have half the fun I did. And Lord Rufton was the most faithful of all; and so he came to live here and now I look after him."

"How kind of Your Grace," Virginia exclaimed. "There are not many people who will look after a friend when they grow old."

"My dear, we must all do our best for other people, must we not?" the Duchess asked.

They were climbing, Virginia noticed, from the first floor up to the second. They went down a long passage, twisting and turning until she felt she would never find her way back alone. Then, at last, they came to a big, mahogany door on which the Duchess knocked.

It was opened by a man in a white coat.

"Good morning, Mr. Warner!" the Duchess said. "How is His Lordship today?"

"We are in very good form today, your Grace. Happy; quiet. We were hoping that your Grace would visit us."

"This is Miss Langholme!" the Duchess said. "Mr. Warner is a fully trained male nurse, Miss Langholme, and I cannot think what we, or, indeed, Lord Rufton, would do without him."

"Your Grace is very kind," Mr. Warner said in self-satisfied tones.

He walked across a small *entresol* and opened another door. In a large, sunlit sitting-room was seated an old man with white hair. He was meticulously and elegantly dressed. There was a flower in his buttonhole and a large diamond and pearl tie-pin in his grey stock. At the sight of the Duchess he rose to his feet and held out his hands.

"Millie, my dear!" he exclaimed.

She rustled towards him. He gave her a royal bow, then he took one of her hands in his and raised it to his lips.

"It is a long time since you have been to see me."

"I know, and it is very naughty of me," the Duchess said. "How well you look this morning."

Mr. Warner had withdrawn from the room and Virginia, feeling a little embarrassed, walked towards the window and looked out. Below her she could see the park where she had ridden with the Duke this morning, and on the lake she could see a flash of white from the little temple of love which was still haunted by the White Lady. The legend had a fascination for her and she wondered how deeply the lady had, in fact, loved the Duke who had died for her sake.

"You sent me that little letter," the Duchess was saying behind her, "but, alas, you forgot to sign it. You know how I treasure your notes, my dear Arthur. Will you put your signature to this one so that I may keep it, as I have kept all your other *billets-doux* through the many years we have known each other?"

"But, of course, dear lady, of course," Lord Rufton agreed.

Virginia looked round. The Duchess was guiding the old man to a writing-table. On it was a big quill pen and she was placing it in his hand.

"Where do I sign it?" Virginia heard him murmur. "I have forgotten what I wrote."

"It was very charming and very sweet," the Duchess said soothingly. "Just your name. Just put on Rufton."

"Rufton?" he queried. "But you always called me Arthur."

"I know, dear," the Duchess said. "But as your note is for posterity I shall want your real name, shall I not?"

"Yes . . . yes, of course," he said. "I had forgotten that my writing is so important."

"Very much so," the Duchess said. "I have them all—those delightful poems. Dear Arthur! How clever you were! Yes, sign there . . . that is it. Thank you very much, indeed."

Lord Rufton sank back in the chair as if he were exhausted. The Duchess took the quill from his hand and put it back beside the ink-pot.

"And now, Miss Langholme and I must leave you," she said.

"Are you going to . . . London?" he asked. "I will come with you. It is a long time . . . since I have been . . . in London."

"Yes, yes, we must go together," the Duchess said. "But not today, not today, Arthur."

She patted his hand and turned towards the door.

"Come, Miss Langholme," she said. "His Lordship is getting tired."

She was holding in her hand the note that Lord Rufton had signed. Virginia glanced at it and then looked again. She could not help feeling that it looked extraordinarily like a cheque. Then she told herself that she must be mistaken and when she looked back the Duchess had whisked the piece of paper—or whatever it might be—out of sight by tucking it into the broad, velvet waistband which was clasped with a filigree silver buckle.

"Goodbye, Mr. Warner!" the Duchess was saying. "I am glad His Lordship is so much better. It has been delightful to see him."

"We haven't had a turn for nearly a month," Mr. Warner said. "The doctor is very gratified, as Your Grace can well believe."

"And so am I, Mr. Warner. It is all due to your kind attention."

"It is very good of Your Grace to say so," Mr. Warner said, bowing low as they passed through the outer door and back into the passage.

"Thank you, dear," the Duchess said to Virginia as they

walked away. "That was very kind of you. And, incidentally, I should not mention where we have been, either to Miss Marshbanks, who is inclined to be jealous, or, indeed, to my son. You see, I never mention Lord Rufton to him if I can help it. He begrudges the fact that the old man has stayed here so long. It is mean of Sebastian because, after all, Lord Rufton was also a devoted friend of my husband's for many years."

Virginia did not speak. She wondered why the Duke, who had seemed so pleasant, so sympathetic, when they were together, should have such a mean and despicable side to his nature when it came to anything concerning money. How little that poor old man must cost compared with the food and servants kept ready at a moment's notice in half a dozen houses.

The Duchess stopped suddenly.

"I think you will find it just as convenient to slip down this way to the library," she said, pointing to another flight of stairs, and Virginia knew she was afraid someone would see them together. "I hope you enjoy your stay with us," she added graciously and passed on towards the Grand Staircase.

Virginia went very slowly down the other stairs. She had an uncomfortable feeling that she had done something wrong. She could not think why, but the feeling persisted. And, beside it, another question nagged at her all the time. Why was the Duke so mean, so parsimonious over money, when he had all her fortune to draw on?

7

VIRGINIA was engrossed in a book which recounted the early history of the Castle when she heard the library door open. She did not turn her head, hoping that whoever it was would not see her and would go away, but a moment later a voice said:

"And how is our pretty little librarian getting on?"

She looked up to see Marcus Ryll smiling at her in a manner which made her feel as if he was mentally undressing her.

"I am very busy, Captain Ryll," she said.

"Not too busy to talk to me, I hope," he rejoined. "I feel that we should have a lot to talk about, you and I."

"I cannot think why," Virginia answered, not in a rude voice, but as one merely stating a fact.

"Well, for one thing, I think you are very attractive," he explained. "And for another, I am very attracted to you."

"I think I should make it clear, Captain Ryll, that I have no time for flirtations," Virginia said firmly.

Even as she spoke she was rather amused at her own handling of the situation. Before her illness she would have been in a flutter at the mere idea of any man, whoever he might be, admiring her. But now, with her new-found consciousness of her own attractiveness, she was not only unimpressed by such obviously insincere protestations, she was also no longer afraid.

Marcus Ryll was quite unabashed.

"Who said anything about flirting?" he asked. "I am speaking the truth. What man would not admire you? And I have the feeling that your demure little schoolgirl pose disguises something quite different. Perhaps you are the Sleeping Beauty. If so, I hope I am going to be the Prince who will awaken you."

Virginia laughed, she could not help it. There was something almost ridiculous about this dressed-up young aristocrat trying to seduce her.

"I am afraid, Captain Ryll, you are going to be very disappointed in me," she said. "American girls are used to looking after themselves. So I assure you that I am no Sleeping Beauty but someone very much awake and alive to what is going on."

Marcus Ryll threw back his head and laughed.

"You are incorrigible," he declared. "And it makes me all the more anxious to interest you in the English way of life, or—should I say?—in one particular Englishman."

"I should have thought you had your hands full already, Captain Ryll," Virginia said demurely.

For a moment he was taken back.

"The servants have been talking, have they?" he asked. "You are referring, of course, to Lady Shelmadine. Well, there is always room in every man's life for another woman, especially when she is as pretty as you."

He put his arm around Virginia's shoulder as he spoke.

"Oh, come on," he said. "Be a sport. Let's have a bit of fun together."

Virginia pushed him away.

"Do not touch me!" she said sharply. "I have a very

rooted objection to being touched by people I do not know. Now, I am busy. Good afternoon, Captain Ryll!"

He was not in the least discouraged but merely amused.

"By Jove! You've got spirit!" he exclaimed. "I always think a woman is a bore if she is too complaisant. A little opposition is like salt to a meal."

"I rather object to being called 'a meal'," Virginia retorted.

She tried to move out of his reach, but in two steps he was at her side and trying once again to put his arms around her.

"Will you leave me alone?" she demanded furiously, and they both heard the library door open.

As they started apart, Virginia felt the colour rise in her cheeks at the interpretation anyone might put on the scene. Even Marcus Ryll looked embarrassed.

It was Lady Shelmadine who entered and there was no doubt, from the look in her face, what she suspected had occurred.

"So, you are here, Marcus!" she said. "I have been looking for you. Good afternoon, Miss Langholme! What a busy little bee you are these days. Out riding with the Duke early in the morning and entertaining Captain Ryll in the library in the afternoon. I suppose American girls do not have to worry about their reputations! After all, you have no Society in America, have you?"

"No, only Red Indians and millionaires!" Virginia said.

"And you fall into neither category," Lady Shelmadine replied. "Oh, well, I dare say it does not matter, but in England we have quite a rude word for young women who push themselves forward."

Virginia took a firm hold of her temper. She knew that Lady Shelmadine was being deliberately provocative and her little chin went up and her eyes flashed. Then she spoke quietly enough:

"It must be difficult for English girls, when married women set them such a strange example."

There was a moment's silence broken by a snigger from Marcus Ryll.

"She's won that round, Shelmadine," he said. "You have to admit that she has spirit."

"I am not interested, Marcus," Lady Shelmadine replied angrily, "in what Miss Langholme has or has not got. I think it is a pity that she does not know her place and perhaps the Duchess should be informed of her behaviour."

She turned round as she spoke, with a little swish of the ruffled and ruched hem of her long skirts, and very elegantly and disdainfully she swept from the library, followed by Captain Ryll who turned at the door to wave his hand at Virginia.

She ignored him but when they had gone she could not help giggling quietly to herself. She might, as Marcus Ryll had said, have spirit, but until now she had never known she possessed it. She was really rather pleased with herself.

"I suppose I have got a quick brain tucked away somewhere," she thought. "And, of course, it is helped by knowing that I am no longer hideous."

Then she felt a little twinge of anxiety. It would be awkward if Lady Shelmadine should actually carry out her threat and complain to the Duchess. She might be asked to leave the Castle before she was ready to go! Virginia admitted to herself that she was intrigued and interested not only by the Castle but also by the Duke—this strange man whom she had married and who seemed full of contradictions, charming one moment, mean and petty another. She might tell herself that she hated him, but she knew she was looking forward to the moment when she would see him again.

The rest of the afternoon passed uneventfully. She saw no one and no one came to the library, but when she was going upstairs to her room to change for dinner she met Miss Marshbanks in the passage, carrying a large board in her hand.

"Are you all right, Miss Langholme?" she asked. "I am sorry I have not been to see you all day but I have been so busy. There is a dinner-party tonight and it always makes a lot of extra work."

"A dinner-party!" Virginia exclaimed. "But I thought you said the Duchess was not entertaining."

"Not in the way we usually do," Miss Marshbanks replied. "And thank goodness Her Grace's mourning is coming to an end! But tonight we have the Judge who is on circuit to dinner. It is traditional, of course, when he comes to the local Assizes, that he should dine here with his Marshal."

"Do tell me what all this means," Virginia begged.

"I will tell you at dinner," Miss Marshbanks replied.

"But now I have got to see to the seating at the table. I have the place-board here."

She showed Virginia what she carried in her hand. It was a board shaped like an oblong table and there were slots for cards to be slipped in, inscribed with the name of a guest.

"This is one of my jobs," Miss Marshbanks explained. "I seat the guests in order of precedence and then if Her Grace wishes to change anyone round she does so. But usually she relies on my judgment. 'I can always trust you to do the right thing, Marshy,' she says."

"How interesting," Virginia said. "And how do you know who are the most important?"

"Oh, in England we have *Debrett*! It is a big book which contains everyone in the Peerage," Miss Marshbanks explained. "I often wonder what I should do without it. Of course, there are only a few really important people coming tonight; the rest are local. Nothing like when we have Royalty at Ryll. Then I really have to be careful that I do not put a foot wrong."

Miss Marshbanks laughed.

"I should get my head cut off if I did, I am quite certain. But I cannot stay here talking to you. I have to get the Duchess to approve this and then send it down to the party so that the place-cards are arranged on the table."

"I should love to see the table when it is finished," Virginia said.

"Then you shall," Miss Marshbanks said graciously. "I will give you a big surprise, but you will have to wait until we have had our own dinner."

She hurried away and Virginia went to her own room. The mere idea of a dinner-party, although she was not going to it, made her feel gay. How few dinner-parties she had been to. She had really been too young before her marriage, but her mother had let her come down to meet the guests before dinner and then, when the meal started, she had been sent up to the school-room.

She had certainly not wanted to sit at the enormous, over-laden table with the Senators, with their booming voices and their overdressed, rather dull wives. She had been conscious that they spoke to her out of duty and behind her back commiserated amongst themselves with her mother for having such an unattractive daughter.

"Tonight I should like to go to the party," Virginia

thought, and wondered what would happen if she walked downstairs and had herself announced as the Duchess of Merrill. She could imagine the astonishment on everyone's face and the fury of Lady Shelmadine. It would be almost worthwhile to do it, if only to enrage the woman who was trying to ensnare her husband.

But why did Lady Shelmadine want the Duke when she was in love with Marcus Ryll? Virginia could not understand it. Was it just a desire for power, to have both men in her clutches? Or was it money? Virginia felt it was unlikely that Lady Shelmadine would be able to extract anything substantial in that respect from the Duke.

She took a dress of white chiffon trimmed with a deep hem of real lace from the wardrobe. It was deceptively simple but had been very expensive.

"It makes you look like a bride," Aunt Ella May had said rather thoughtlessly, and feeling that she might hurt her aunt if she refused to buy the dress on that score, Virginia had included it with her other purchases.

She put it on now and wondered how it would look with a diamond necklace round her neck and a tiara in her pale hair. Then she remembered the terrible tiara she had worn on her wedding day—that ghastly, hideous crown that her mother had thought befitted her new position in life.

"Poor Mama!" Virginia whispered to herself. "She did not understand even the beginnings of good taste."

Ever since she had come to the Castle, Virginia knew that the beauty of the place, the antique furniture, the pictures, the carved woodwork, and the painted ceilings, all gave her an aesthetic sense of joy just because they were so beautiful. Everywhere she looked there was beauty—the beauty which came from age and from the loving care of hands down the centuries. Not all the money in America, she thought, could create a house as magnificent and fine as Ryll Castle.

She went down to dinner. She and Miss Marshbanks dined by candlelight as they had done before. The food was delicious and the footman brought them a bottle of champagne in a great silver ice-bucket.

"I usually have champagne when there is a party," Miss Marshbanks said with a little touch of pride in her voice.

Virginia, remembering the champagne her mother had forced on her before her wedding, felt a sudden nausea at the very thought of it. Then she sensed that to refuse to drink with Miss Marshbanks would be to spoil some of the older woman's pleasure.

"It is a great treat," she managed to say and knew that Miss Marshbanks was delighted at her appreciation.

When they finished the meal Miss Marshbanks said:

"And now I am going to give you another treat. Follow me, but you must be very quiet. When we get to the door to the Oak Gallery I want you to take off your shoes."

Miss Marshbanks, leading the way towards the dining-room, opened a small door giving off the passage, and slipping off her shoes indicated to Virginia to do the same. They went tiptoeing up a staircase which ended in a small, oak-panelled room with one wall comprised of carved pillars set only a few inches apart. It was a minstrels' gallery and the chairs for the musicians were still in place.

As Miss Marshbanks crept towards the carved pillars, Virginia suddenly realised why they must be quiet. The gallery was at one end of the Great Banqueting Hall. They could see but not be seen, and below them the Duke and his mother were entertaining their guests.

For a moment Virginia could only see a kaleidoscope of graceful, naked shoulders, glittering tiaras and flashing necklaces. Then, beside the ladies, she observed the distinguished-looking men, seated around a table laden with gold candelabra and decorated with flowers. There was smilax trailing over the white tablecloth; in the centre there was a huge, gold vase and on either side of it bowls of hot-house fruit.

The whole picture was one of colour and animation. Powdered footmen in velvet uniforms trimmed with gold stood behind every chair. Cut-crystal wine glasses glistened in the light from the candles.

Instinctively Virginia's eyes went to the Duke at the end of the table. For a moment she could only think how handsome he looked, and then she saw that on his right there was an extremely pretty brunette with a magnificent necklace of rubies and diamonds round her neck and a tiara to match. On his left was Lady Shelmadine.

As Virginia watched, Lady Shelmadine leaned forward and put her hand on the Duke's arm. She was obviously pleading with him about something, for her face was turned up to his, her red mouth pouting provocatively. Virginia felt she could almost see the enticement in her slanting green eyes.

Suddenly the room seemed to swim before her. Why should she be watching in secret, peeping through the pillars, when her place was down below? Then she forced herself to remember that she hated this man who had married her for two million dollars. It was doubtless her money that was paying for the food which they ate off the gold plates; her money which provided the wines; her money which paid the footmen.

She shut her eyes as if she could bear no more and, turning away, walked down the stairs from the minstrels' gallery and back down the passage to the sitting-room she shared with Miss Marshbanks.

"Why did you leave?" Miss Marshbanks said, hurrying in a little while later. "I wanted to point out to you who was there. Did you not think Lady Roehampton looked magnificent? She was seated on the Duke's right and is one of the great beauties of England. I should have liked you also to notice Lady Preston; she is half French and they say that no man can resist her."

"It was very kind of you to take me," Virginia assured her. "Thank you very much. But if you will forgive me now, I want some fresh air."

She slipped away before Miss Marshbanks could say any more and finding her way to the garden door went out, closing it behind her. She had one idea and that was to get away from the Castle and what she had seen in the Grand Banqueting Hall. She did not know why, but she did not want to hear about them—those lovely women with their Society background, their beauty and their jewels.

"I shall go back to America in a few days," Virginia told herself. "I have nothing in common with this sort of life. I shall ask Aunt Ella May to find me something to do. I might teach in a school, or I might breed horses."

She supposed, although she had never asked, that she still owned her father's ranch in Texas. It might be a good idea to go there and find out what was happening to the great herds of cattle he had possessed. Then she wondered how she could ever do it alone.

Without realising where her feet had carried her she found herself in the tree-shaded glade, sitting on the seat and looking at the statue of the dancing faun. Beyond was the lake. Already the darkness was falling and the stars were coming out in the sky.

"I must go back to America!" Virginia said aloud, but already the tranquillity of this secret place was creeping over her. She no longer felt agitated; she no longer wanted to run away. The beauty of it captured her senses—the blue mist over the water, the branches of the trees silhouetted against the sky, the soft noises from the wood—a bird going to roost, a rabbit scampering over the leaves. The peace of it seemed to embrace her and she surrendered herself to its magic.

It must have been a very long time later when she realised she was not alone. She could not see him but she knew he was there. She wondered how long he had been watching her without her being aware of it.

The moon had risen over the trees and, as if the little clearing in which she sat had been designed for that very purpose, it shone upon her, illuminating her white dress, her hair and her little pointed face. She looked towards him and instantly he moved, coming from the shadows into the moonlight.

"I was afraid you were only a figment of my imagination," he said, his voice very low as if something had disturbed him.

"I feel rather unreal," Virginia replied. "As I sat here thinking, the world seemed very far away."

The Duke sat down beside her.

"Of what were you thinking?" he asked.

"I was wondering if dying was as difficult as living," Virginia said.

"Do you find living difficult?" he inquired.

She nodded her head.

"In a way. One is frightened and yet fascinated. I think one is always anxious in case one might miss something; that life can go too quickly and will have passed you by."

"You sound very, very old," he said with a hint of laughter in his voice.

"On the contrary, I think I am very, very young," Virginia rejoined, "and I do not really understand living—at least not as the Castle understands it and, perhaps, some English people."

He understood what she was trying to say.

"The Castle is ageless," he said. "It is made up of generations of Rylls; but each one of them struggled and fought to be an individual, each one of them was happy and unhappy, each one of them, at times, felt frustrated and that they were missing something—like you."

Virginia gave a little laugh.

"You make things seem so much better," she said. "I

think really I was overpowered by the age of it all, but, then, I come from a very new country."

"I should like to show you so much more of England than just this," he said.

"Nevertheless, 'this', as you call it, is very interesting to an American," Virginia said. "I watched you at dinner tonight and, I do not know why, but somehow it upset me."

"You watched me?" the Duke asked. Then he smiled: "I know, the minstrels' gallery! I used to go there when I was a child and whenever there was a big party, Matthews would give me titbits from the dinner and always some of the special chocolates and peppermints from the dishes on the table."

"You love the Castle, do you not?" Virginia asked.

"I am part of it," the Duke answered simply.

"And you would do anything to keep it?" Virginia said. "Anything?"

"Perhaps," she thought to herself, "this is the secret of why he wanted my money."

There was a pause before the Duke replied.

"I look on the Castle as a heritage," he explained, "something very precious that has been lent to me and which I must hand over intact and in good repair to my heirs."

He spoke very seriously. Then his mood changed.

"I did not come here to talk about the Castle," he said. "I came to find you. I was half afraid you would not have waited for me."

"But I was not waiting for you," Virginia said. "I just did not realise the time."

Even as she spoke she wondered if it was the truth, if, even subconsciously, she knew that the Duke would come to her if she came to this secret place.

"I ran, Virginia, hoping you would be here."

"You wanted to see me?"

The moonlight was on her face and he could see the question in her eyes.

"You know I wanted to see you," he said. "I have been wanting to all day. I think, Virginia, you have bewitched me."

For a moment she could not answer him, before with an effort, she turned her face away.

"I am sure that is not true," she said. "It is just that

perhaps I am a little different because I am an American."

"You are different," he said, and a low, caressing note in his voice seemed to vibrate across her senses. "Very different from any woman I have ever known before. It is not only that you are so lovely—and you are very lovely—it is because I like talking to you, I like being with you, and when you are not there everything seems to go flat."

"I . . . I somehow feel that you ought not to be talking . . . to me . . . like this," Virginia murmured.

"Why not?" he asked. "Oh, my dear! Do not be frightened of me. I will not do you any harm. But I have the feeling, in fact I know, that from the very moment I saw you I fell in love!"

"It . . . is not . . . true!" Virginia exclaimed.

"It is the truth," he declared. "I did not mean to tell you. I meant to keep our relationship on a friendly basis. I felt that was what you wanted. But I cannot help myself, Virginia. All day I have been in a kind of dream because we were together this morning. I knew when we first met yesterday—Heavens! it seems a century ago!—that something strange had happened. And then this morning when I saw you at Queen's Heart I knew. I knew when I watched your profile silhouetted against the sky as you stood at the balustrade, and then as you moved and looked at me my heart turned over. What have you done to me, Virginia? Why should I feel like this?"

"You are imagining it," Virginia said, and her voice was frightened.

"How easy if I could dismiss it as something I have imagined," the Duke said. "But we would both be liars if we did not admit that such a thing as love at first sight does exist in the world. I have read about it; I have laughed at it; I have thought it ridiculous. But, Virginia, it has happened to me!"

"I wonder what you mean by love?" Virginia asked.

"I mean," the Duke replied, and his voice was deep with sincerity, "that it is love when you know you have found the other half of yourself, the person to whom you belong and who belongs to you, the person for whom you have been searching all your life."

Virginia felt as if it were hard for her to breathe. There was something in his voice that seemed to stir every nerve in her body. He had not attempted to touch her and yet she felt as if he held her close against him. It was almost as if he hypnotised her. She could not move. He was close, so close. She felt as if, in fact, she did belong to him.

Then, thrusting herself back into the real world, she remembered why she was here.

"How can you talk of love when . . . we hardly know each other?" she asked, and even to herself her voice sounded weak and vacillating.

"Do you not know me?" he asked. "Then that, darling, is something I must teach you. For I know a great deal about you. I know you are everything a man wants in a woman. I love not only your body but your mind, your kind heart, and the way your sense of the ridiculous breaks through when you are trying to be very solemn and serious."

He paused, then continued:

"If I were an artist I could paint a picture of you. If I were a musician I could write a concerto and it would be you. Is that not love, Virginia?"

"I do . . . not know," she said helplessly.

"Then that is what I am going to teach you," he said. "Think of the days we have before us, Virginia, when we can be together. We can ride over to Queen's Heart in the morning and we can come here in the evening. I can show you the estate and, beyond that, the county, and perhaps later, London. Let me be your teacher, for I have never in the whole of my life had so much of such importance to teach."

Virginia drew a deep breath and turning to face him she said:

"And what happens at the end?"

She could see that he was taken aback at her question but he hesitated for only a second.

"Why should there be an end?" he inquired.

"There will be," she persisted. "Everything comes to an end."

"Not love," he said firmly. "Love can go on and on. This is only a beginning, Virginia. It is like opening the first page of a book and knowing there are hundreds of pages ahead, all more exciting and more thrilling than the one we are looking at now."

"But still there will be an end," she repeated.

"Can we not face that difficulty when we come to it?" he asked. "Let us just think about ourselves; what we mean to each other. I love you, Virginia. Will you trust me?"

He put out his hand but she did not take it.

"I will not force you," he said quietly. "I know that I have spoken too soon. I know I should have waited to let you get used to me. But you go to my head. You entrance and exhilarate me and I cannot help telling you that I love you!"

Virginia rose to her feet. Very slowly, with the moonlight on her, she walked down the soft glade towards the little faun. When she reached the statue she stood beside it, touching with her hand the small bronze head. It was cold beneath her touch.

"It is Eros, the God of Love!" the Duke said softly. "It was brought here from Greece by one of my ancestors. I think perhaps he directed you to this very special spot."

Still Virginia said nothing, her eyes downcast, her head bent a little. And after a moment the Duke said:

"You know that I long to kiss you! You know that it drives me almost insane to watch you and not to put my arms around you. But I do not want to frighten you. I want you to come to me and love me, as I love you. Think about me, Virginia. Promise me that you will think about me."

She smiled a little at that.

"I doubt if I could help doing that," she replied.

"Oh, my darling! It makes me so happy to hear you say that. I want to be with you in your thoughts from the very first moment you awake until the moment you fall asleep. And you know that wherever you are, whatever you are doing, I shall be thinking of you, longing for you, wanting you!"

There was a sudden passion in his voice which made Virginia turn away.

"We must go back," she said quietly. "It must be very late."

"Will you ride with me tomorrow morning?" the Duke asked.

"Will it not make people talk if we do?" she asked.

"Damn them! What does it matter?" the Duke rejoined. "They can talk if they wish, as far as I am concerned. But I would not want to make it uncomfortable for you."

"I do not mind," Virginia said. "I do not belong here, as you do."

"Then we ride together," he said. "I will wait for you at six o'clock, as I did this morning."

They walked back towards the Castle in silence. Yet,

somehow, Virginia felt that in their very silence they were closer than they had been before. Then she told herself that was a ridiculous notion. He might make love to her but she knew him for what he was. She was not a child to be beguiled by pretty words. She might feel as if she were mesmerised by him when they were together, but she knew, as no one else would have known, that he was not to be trusted.

They reached the outskirts of the garden.

"We will go in by separate doors," the Duke said. "I think you came through the garden-door, is that right?"

Virginia nodded.

"Very well," he said. "For the sake of appearances—I'm sure people have been wondering where I am—I'm going in the other way. Good night, Virginia. I shall not sleep. I shall lie awake counting the hours until I see you again. It will seem like an eternity until tomorrow morning."

"Good night!" Virginia replied, and then, as she would have left him, he caught her hand and held her back.

"Tell me you are not angry with me," he pleaded. "Tell me I have not shocked or frightened you. Tell me that you think somewhere in your heart you might be a little interested in me."

She would have spoken, but he interrupted her.

"No, do not say it," he commanded. "Leave me for a moment in my fool's paradise, believing you like me a little bit and that I am, at least, a friend. Good night, my darling, my beautiful, my own American!"

He raised her hand to his mouth and she felt his lips, warm and passionate, against the palm. Then he had moved away into the shadows, walking quickly as a man who dare not hesitate lest he should turn back.

Giving a heavy sigh as if from the very depths of her being, she crossed the lawn, keeping in the shadows of the trees to reach the side of the house. She was just about to walk in front of a French window when, suddenly, a light shone out and almost beside her the window was flung open and a voice said:

"It is very hot in here. I cannot think why you have dragged me downstairs at this time of night."

Instinctively, Virginia pressed herself back against the side of the house. She knew the voice all too well. It was Lady Shelmadine.

"I have to talk to you," she heard Marcus Ryll say, "and it would have been madness for me to come to your room.

You never know who is snooping about the passages."

"Well, what is it?" Lady Shelmadine asked almost sharply. "If anyone finds us here they are not going to believe the hoary old excuse that I came down in the middle of the night to choose a book."

"Wait a minute. Let me light these candles," Marcus Ryll said.

The light from the window looked more brilliant from outside. Virginia glanced over her shoulder. There was no retreat. Another window of the same room was behind her and whichever way she moved she would be bound to be seen.

"Is something really wrong?"

Lady Shelmadine's voice was anxious.

"Wrong! It could not be more disastrous. I had a letter by this evening's post. I could not tell you before——as a matter of fact I did not read it until I went upstairs to dress for dinner. I knew there would be something unpleasant in it!"

"What did it say?" Lady Shelmadine asked.

"I have got exactly a week in which to find the money!"

"All of it?"

"All of it! The whole damned forty thousand quid!"

"But it is impossible!"

"Of course it is, absolutely and completely impossible! And there's no staving them off this time."

"You will have to go to Sebastian," Lady Shelmadine said.

"Do you think he would give me forty thousand? He told me last time he would never pay up for me again, and he certainly would not produce a sum like that."

"He will have to! You cannot go to prison."

"It is either prison or I leave the country. I shall never be able to come back."

There was a pause.

"There is another alternative, of course," Lady Shelmadine said.

"You mean the pills?"

"Yes, you brought them with you, did you not?"

"I am not likely to be such a damned fool as to leave them about. They are lethal—at least that is what the chap said."

"My friend who gave me his address said they never fail," Lady Shelmadine said. "He used them in East Africa and the result was instantaneous."

"I know, Shelmadine, but I cannot quite stomach doing a thing like this; not to Sebastian."

"He stands in your way, does he not?" Lady Shelmadine asked. "He is hard and heartless. There is nothing more I can do where he is concerned. I have tried everything. I do not think he is quite human; and, at any rate, you would make a much more amusing Duke!"

"You're a devil, aren't you, Shelmadine?" Marcus Ryll asked. "It is always the woman who is more ruthless, when it comes to the point, than any man."

"It is up to you," Lady Shelmadine replied. "If you prefer to go to prison how can I stop you! They will not be very pleasant about that cheque you forged. The penalties are pretty stiff for forgeries I am told."

"Stop it, Shelmadine!" Marcus Ryll cried. "All right! We have no alternative, have we? You are quite certain there is no way of tracing the poison?"

"All you have to do is to put one tablet in his coffee or his wine," Lady Shelmadine said. "Do not do it, of course, when you are alone together. If he dies you do not want to be the only witness. It ought not to be too difficult."

There was a long pause.

"You have got them here, I suppose? You are not lying to me?" Lady Shelmadine asked.

"No, no, they are upstairs in a drawer of the dressing-table. But I do not like it. I may be a cad in some ways, but I have never before really contemplated murder!"

"All right, then! Do as you please, but do not expect me either to visit you in prison or to scuttle across the Channel to live in penury in some foreign slum. There are other men in the world!"

"Shelmadine! I will do what you say! There is no other way out."

"Then it is agreed," Lady Shelmadine said. "Now, for heaven's sake let me go back to bed. If we are caught here somebody might be suspicious."

"And you will marry me, Shelmadine, when it is all over?"

There was a little gurgle of laughter.

"I have always wanted to be a Duchess! and of course, Marcus, diamonds are very becoming!"

There was the sound of a door opening.

"Here, Shelmadine, wait! You cannot go like that." A door closed. "Damn the woman! I suppose I am left to tidy up."

Marcus Ryll came to the French windows to close them. The lights were extinguished, one by one, until Virginia guessed that he was left with only a candle in his hand. Then there was darkness!

Virginia realised she was trembling and the full import of what she had heard swept over her as if she had been doused in cold water. It was not possible! She must have been dreaming! People did not do such things. She could not believe what she had heard.

Then she knew that no one would believe her if she reported the conversation that she had just overheard. If she went to the Duke at this moment he would laugh at her. No one would credit that two members of the aristocracy would be capable of such a crime. It would be her word against theirs and who was likely to believe an unknown girl from America?

Slowly she moved along the side of the house. She opened the door from the garden and, to her relief, found it was still unlocked. Slowly she went up a side staircase to her bedroom. The room looked warm, cosy and secure. The flowered chintz, the soft-pile carpet, the elegant furniture, were part of the Castle, part of the secure background of the English aristocracy.

A crime was about to be committed—a crime so horrible that she could hardly bear to think of it. And yet she knew she was powerless. No one would believe her and because of this the Duke would die!

She thought of him taking the poison. She thought of him dying. Yet her hands were tied and she could not prevent it. Then, as she cried out at the horror of it, she knew that she loved him.

8

ALL night long Virginia tossed and turned or lay staring into the darkness, bewildered by her thoughts and feelings. She knew that somehow she must save the Duke, not only because she loved him but because never in her wildest dreams had she imagined that murder was so easy or could be premeditated by people like Marcus Ryll and Lady Shelmadine. The sheer beastliness of it was difficult for her to understand. She knew that she must stop it whatever the consequences to herself—and yet the question was, how?

She could not imagine herself telling the Duke that his cousin was plotting to murder him. She could almost see the look of amusement and incredulity on his face. And even if he believed her what could he do about it? Accuse Marcus and reveal that his conversation at night with Lady Shelmadine had been overheard by an unknown American girl?

She could hear their laughter at the very absurdity of such an idea. And if she told someone else, someone outside the family—a solicitor, a doctor, or even someone connected with the police—it would be quite impossible for them to act until it was too late. Then they could only say that she had been right, and what consolation would that be?

How ever she looked at it, no solution to the problem seemed to present itself. All that she could do would be to wait until the Duke was dead and then denounce Marcus Ryll for the villain he was.

She shut her eyes and felt herself tremble again at the Duke's words. She had not believed it was possible to vibrate to a man's voice, and yet she knew, now, that he had only to be beside her, only to speak to her in that deep voice which seemed to hide a subdued passion behind every word, for her to feel as if every nerve in her body was alive and pulsating for him.

She had known as they sat side by side on the seat in the glade that if he had put out his hands and touched her she would have been unable to resist him. Gone was her pride, her reserve and her hatred. That was the extraordinary thing—that he had turned her vivid, vehement hatred against him into a love that would not be denied. Her brain still tried to reiterate that he was a deceiver and a fortune-hunter, but her body betrayed her. She wanted him, ached for him!

She found herself whispering over and over again the things he had said to her. She found herself remembering every little movement he had made. She found herself reliving the ride they had taken together, that moment on the terrace at Queen's Heart when she had known that he was attracted by her.

And yet some small part of her brain, critical and aloof, asked, "How much does his love mean? How deep and how enduring would it be? Is it, in fact, just the infatuation of a spoilt and passionate man for a new and pretty face?"

At last she could torture herself no longer with the questions that beset her. After hours of soul-searching she was no nearer to a solution of the problem which mattered above all else—how could she save the Duke's life.

There had been no pretence about the manner in which Marcus Ryll and Lady Shelmadine had talked of disposing of him. There had been a stark deliberateness about their tones which convinced Virginia that there was no doubt at all that they would put their plan into operation.

She got out of bed and drew back the curtains from the window. Dawn was just breaking in the east. The sable of the sky was fading and the stars showed only a faint twinkle in the highest part of the heavens. There was a mist drifting over the lake and encircling the trunks of the trees in the park. A flight of wild duck came in through the mist and vanished into the sunrise.

It was all calm and tranquil. The great oak trees that had stood for hundreds of years seemed like sentinels against the brutality of man. There was peace here, and the first songs of the birds made it seem impossible that ruthless intrigues could ever destroy the security and serenity of this very English scene.

"Perhaps I have dreamed it all," Virginia whispered to herself. "Perhaps my mind has imagined what it heard."

A sudden movement beneath her window made her bend forward and she saw, directly down below, Marcus Ryll come down the steps of the house and walk towards the stables. He was wearing riding-breeches and carrying a whip, and she knew, then, that someone else had been unable to sleep, someone else had tossed and turned and perhaps grappled with his conscience all night.

She glanced at the clock on the mantelpiece. It was nearly five o'clock. Too early for anyone else in the house to be awake, but, doubtless, Marcus Ryll would arouse some stable-boy from his slumbers and require him to saddle a horse.

She stood for a moment watching him out of sight and then, suddenly, she knew what she must do. She picked up her dressing-gown from where it lay on a chair at the foot of the bed. It was a robe of heavy, white *crêpe de Chine* trimmed with Valenciennes lace. She slipped into it and pulled the cord tight around her waist.

It was dangerous but she knew there was no other course! She opened her door very quietly. The passage outside was in darkness and she moved along it, her soft-soled bedroom slippers making no sound on the thick carpet.

It was quite a distance from her room to the first-floor landing, where the more important guest-rooms opened on to the wide corridor to which the Great Staircase led. She knew which was Marcus Ryll's room because as she came up the stairs after luncheon the previous day, he had emerged and smiled his lecherous smile at the sight of her. Fortunately she had been accompanied by Miss Marshbanks, so he had not been able to engage her in conversation.

The landing at the top of the Great Staircase was lit by the first pale rays of the dawn coming through the high, stained-glass windows in the hall. It was very quiet. There could be heard only the tick-tick of the grandfather clock and the voices of the birds outside. Virginia slipped into the shadows against Marcus Ryll's door. For a moment, as she touched the handle, she hesitated and felt her heart almost stop beating with fear.

Supposing she had been mistaken! Supposing that in some extraordinary way he had managed to slip back from the stables and was inside his bedroom! What would he think at the sight of her? What, indeed, would he say? But she knew her own position in the matter was of no consequence. It was the Duke who mattered! The Duke who must be saved at all costs!

Very, very softly she turned the handle. The curtains were drawn back from the windows, but the room was empty. The bed was in confusion, a testimony to the fact that she had been right in her assumption that Marcus Ryll had been unable to sleep. His pyjamas were lying on the floor.

Virginia had eyes for only one thing—the chest of drawers that she saw was used as a dressing-table, with the small, mahogany swinging mirror above it and Marcus Ryll's ivory hair-brushes laid out beside a case containing his razors.

Swiftly she crossed the room and pulled open a drawer. It contained socks, ties, handkerchiefs but nothing else. She tried another. Here were some letters, a leather collar-box, a stud-box, and a small, flat, tin box. Nothing that she was looking for. She imagined the pills would be contained in a white pill-box such as was habitually used by chemists.

She stared at the open drawer in perplexity. She

remembered Marcus saying quite clearly that the poison was in a drawer of the dressing-table. She stared around the room. There was a tallboy in one corner, a writing-desk, several tables—nothing else which could be called a dressing-table.

Then she drew from the back of the drawer the tin box and saw it was old and battered. There was inscribed on it, almost erased by use, the words *First-Aid,* and below them a red cross. She guessed that this was the type of first-aid kit that Marcus Ryll might have carried in the Army and certainly when he was on active service.

She opened it and knew at the first glance that she had found what she sought. The box contained bandages, a pair of scissors and some small bottles. But in the centre was a pill-box, exactly as she had anticipated. She took it out and saw that it contained four small, white pills. She was certain, then, that this was the poison of which Marcus Ryll and Lady Shelmadine had spoken. Four pills and each of them strong enough to kill a man! She had found them!

She closed the first-aid box, replaced it where she had found it and closed the drawer. Then, hastily, with the box containing the pills in her hand, she tiptoed across the room. Now to get back to her own bedroom undetected and destroy the pills before they could do any harm!

She opened the door of the bedroom, stepped into the passage and closed it behind her. Then she stood transfixed! Coming down the corridor was the Duke, dressed in riding-breeches and holding by a lead the Duchess's old, rheumaticky pug, Dizzy.

For a moment he did not see Virginia. He was looking ahead of him almost sightlessly, like a man preoccupied with his inner thoughts. Then, when he was almost upon her, he saw her. She stood there as if turned to stone, the pill-box in her hands, and raised her face, very white and frightened, towards him.

For a few seconds he stared at her incredulously. Then the blood receded from his face, leaving him almost as deathly pale as she was. His eyes moved and he seemed to take in every detail of her appearance—the long, white dressing-gown, her hair falling over her shoulders almost to her waist, her eyes dark with an expression which a man could only interpret as surprise and horror.

For a long, long moment neither of them moved. When

the Duke spoke, his voice was harsh and there was an anger beneath his words which, nevertheless, were controlled as if by an iron will.

"So this is where your interests lie, Miss Langholme!"

Virginia felt as if he had lashed at her with his whip.

"I thought you were different from other women," he went on, "but I see I was mistaken. So it is my cousin who holds the key to your affections. How blind can a man be not to see what is happening under his very nose?"

He was silent, and now Virginia was trembling so violently that the pill-box fell from her hand and spilled on the floor. With an effort she found her voice.

"I . . . I would . . . explain . . ." she began in a broken whisper, but the Duke moved away.

"I think, Miss Langholme," he said, "you have strained my hospitality to its utmost and your departure can be arranged later in the day."

As he turned towards the stairs, Virginia put out her hand towards him.

"Wait!" she pleaded.

The Duke could not move quickly because the pug was straining at the lead. Before he could hold him, the old dog pulled himself towards one of the white pills which had fallen from the box and rolled near him. He gobbled it up and then, pulled by the Duke towards the staircase, he waddled a few steps. Suddenly he gave a strangled grunt, a tremor shook his body and he collapsed, rolling slowly over on to his back, with his legs in the air.

The Duke, checked on the first step of the stairs, turned his head to see what was happening. Hastily picking up the other three pills and placing them in the box, Virginia found her voice.

"That," she said, "that was . . . meant for you!"

"What do you mean?" The Duke's question was sharp.

"These pills," she said, holding them out towards him, "they were to kill you. That . . . was why I stole them. To . . . to save you."

The Duke bent down, released the lead from the pug's collar and, stepping round the dead dog, went to her side. He looked down into her face and gripped her by the shoulders.

"Tell me the truth," he said roughly. "What were you doing in that bedroom?"

His fingers bit into the softness of her skin, but now she was unafraid.

"It is the truth," she answered. "They . . . they meant to kill you. I knew you would not believe me and so I . . . stole the pills."

The Duke looked down into her face searchingly, desperately, seeking the truth. As if what he saw reassured him, he looked up and down the corridor.

"We cannot talk here," he said. He put his hand under her elbow and guided her a short way from where they were standing. He opened a door, drew her inside, shut and locked the door behind them.

Virginia saw they were in a small sitting-room which she guessed was a *boudoir* belonging to one of the grand suites used by the more distinguished guests to the Castle. It was a delightful room, furnished with a soft shade of pink, and, although the room was not in use, the air was fragrant from the flowers arranged on the sidetables—as Virginia had learned from Miss Marshbanks was customary.

The Duke strode across the room and pulled back the curtains. The light flooded in. Then he turned to where Virginia stood just inside the door, her face still very pale, her eyes troubled.

"Now, tell me what all this means," he commanded.

She moved slowly towards him, the pill-box in her hand.

"Last night, when I . . . I left you . . ." she began in a low voice, and then, not looking directly at him because it embarrassed her to tell him such things about the people he knew and trusted, she told him what she had overheard.

"Why did you not come to me?" he asked when she had finished.

For the first time she looked up into his face.

"Would you have believed me?" she asked. "Would you not have thought I was just a stranger making trouble? Or someone whose imagination had run riot?"

"You are right," he said honestly. "It would have been difficult to credit such a story. Even now, even with the dog lying dead outside, it is hard for me to believe that Marcus would really stoop to murder."

"Why could you not give him the money?" Virginia asked. "If he fails this time he may try again."

"I cannot give him such a large amount," the Duke replied. "Even if I could, what would be the use? This has happened a dozen times before in the past; it will go on happening in the future. There is no end to his greed, no end to his stupidity."

He bent forward and took the pill-box from Virginia.

"One thing we can do," he said, "is play for time."

"How?" Virginia asked.

The Duke opened the box and looked at the pills.

"I have some quite harmless tablets in my bedroom," he replied, "which the doctor gave me a long time ago when I had a fever. I can substitute them for these, and for the moment, at any rate, Marcus will wonder why they are not working."

"He has only a week in which to find the money," Virginia said.

"The fool! The stupid fool!" the Duke exclaimed in a sudden anger. "He swore to me on the Bible last time that he would not gamble again. I paid up his debts with money I could ill afford and now, in under six months, he is in the same position that he was in before."

"Then what can you do?" Virginia asked.

"I do not know," the Duke answered. "Perhaps I could face him with the accusation that I know what he was attempting. But that might involve you, and that I could not allow."

"I should not mind," Virginia replied. "Not if it would save your life."

She spoke without thinking and then felt the colour rise in her cheeks as she saw the Duke's eyes go towards her inquiringly.

"Virginia!" he said, and now his tone was very different. "Can you forgive me for what I said to you just now? I do not think you will ever know what it meant to me to see you coming from that man's bedroom; to see you looking as you are now with your wonderful hair falling over your shoulders. If you only knew how much I have longed to see it like that."

"I . . . I think perhaps I . . . ought to go back to my room . . ." Virginia began, and then could say no more for the Duke's hands were once again on her shoulders, holding her prisoner.

"Why did you try to save me?" he asked. "I have to know the answer to that."

His face was very near to hers and she felt a sudden shyness.

"Answer me," he demanded.

She could not find her voice. It seemed to have died in her throat. She was conscious only of the touch of his hands, the nearness of him. She could feel herself quiver and tremble. There was a strange constriction in her throat.

"Look at me, Virginia," the Duke said, and his voice was low and compelling. "Look at me," he repeated with a masterfulness that would not be denied.

Slowly, as if she must obey the authority he had over her, she raised her eyes to his. For a long, long moment they stared at each other and the world seemed to vibrate and move almost dizzily around them. And then suddenly, with an inarticulate sound, the Duke's control broke. He swept Virginia into his arms, his mouth seeking hers.

"Oh, my darling . . . my sweet . . . my love," he murmured. "You cared enough for me to save me. You cared! That is all that matters. Oh, my God! Virginia, I love you!"

He was kissing her wildly—her lips, her eyes, her neck, her hair. She felt as if his passion swept over her like a flood-tide and she surrendered herself to him, knowing that the flame in him had ignited a flame within herself and that their kisses joined them so that they were no longer two people, but one . . .

After what seemed an eternity, after the world had stood still and everything was forgotten but themselves, they came back to reality.

"I must let you go," the Duke said hoarsely. "Oh, Virginia, I never realised love could be like this!"

He still held her closely in his arms and now she rested her head against his shoulder and he looked down at her parted lips, at her flushed cheeks, at her eyes dark with the passion he had evoked in her.

"You are beautiful!" he murmured, "more beautiful than I believed any woman could be. But I must leave you before the house is astir. I must change over the tablets. I must find servants and explain to them that Dizzy has died of a heart attack. It was fortunate that I heard him scratching at my Mother's door to be let out."

"Yes . . . you must do . . . all those . . . things," Virginia said, her voice husky and the words she spoke somehow meaningless beside the fact that she spoke them for him.

"I love you! I love you!" the Duke cried.

He kissed her again, a long, lingering kiss, and she clung to him like a child who has been frightened in the dark but has found security and protection.

"We must go, my darling," he said. "We must talk

together later in the day. But I think for the moment it would not be wise to let Marcus know that his plot has failed."

"No, no! Because he will try something else!" Virginia cried in a sudden terror.

"And next time you may not be able to save me," the Duke said. "I still cannot realise that it is entirely due to you that I am alive. Oh, my sweet, somehow I will repay you."

"I only want you to remain alive," Virginia whispered.

He kissed her again until, at last, as if he could hardly bear to do so, he took his arms from her.

"I will not look at you," he said, "otherwise I shall be unable to go."

He walked across the room and unlocked the door. He looked down the passage.

"There is no one about," he said. "Go back to your room quietly and try to rest. We had best not go riding this morning, for I have things to see to."

"No, of course, I understand," Virginia agreed. But she was disappointed.

She slipped past him, feeling him press his lips against her hair, and then she was speeding down the corridor without looking back. In her own room she flung herself down on the bed, trembling with an irrepressible joy and wonder, conscious only that the hunger of the Duke's lips was still bruising her own.

"He loves me and I love him," she told herself. Then she knew that that same, critical, cynical voice at the back of her brain was in motion. "How much?" it asked, "how much exactly do you mean to him?"

It was terribly difficult to go downstairs to breakfast, to find Miss Marshbanks already waiting, chattering away about her plans for the day.

"I have to go to the village immediately after breakfast," she said. "Is there anything I can collect for you?"

"Do you go every morning?" Virginia asked, and was surprised to see a rather repressed look cross Miss Marshbanks' face.

"Not every morning," she said evasively, "only if Her Grace has something special for me to do there."

Virginia would like to have asked questions but instinctively she knew they would not be welcome.

"Whatever can there be secret about Miss Marshbanks

going to the village?" she asked herself. "I really am imagining things! I am finding plots and intrigues where they are not at all likely to be!"

Breakfast over, she picked up her notebook and conscientiously went to the library, but she found herself utterly unable to concentrate. The books which had seemed a sheer delight the day before were now dull and lifeless. They were full of the past; she was now concerned only with the present and the future.

She wondered what the Duke was doing. She wondered if Marcus Ryll had already inserted one of the fake pills in his coffee at breakfast or whether he was keeping it for the wine at luncheon. At last she put the books back in their places in the bookcases and sat drawing aimlessly on her writing-pad.

She had meant to write to Aunt Ella May, but what could she say? "I have met my husband and fallen in love with him. He is in danger of being murdered." Aunt Ella May would think she was demented.

She was sitting disconsolately staring at the faces she had drawn on her pad when the door opened and the Duchess came in.

"Oh, Miss Langholme!" she said. "I thought I might find you here."

"Good morning, Your Grace!" Virginia said, getting hastily to her feet. "I was trying to work."

"Yes, yes, of course," the Duchess said. "I hope you are finding all you want in the library. But I wonder if you could do something for me?"

"Yes, of course," Virginia answered. "What is it?"

"I have sent Miss Marshbanks to the village," the Duchess said, "and I wish very much for someone to overtake her. I have a message of the utmost urgency. I wonder if it would be asking too much of you to ride after her and prevent her doing what I have asked her to do."

"Yes, of course," Virginia said, feeling a little bewildered and wondering why she should do this when there were so many servants in the Castle.

As if she guessed her thoughts, the Duchess glanced towards the door which she had left ajar.

"I am sure you will understand, Miss Langholme, that this is a very private matter between myself and Miss Marshbanks. I could send a groom; but I do not wish to do that, nor, as it happens, do I wish my son to know that

Miss Marshbanks has gone to the village. He is, of course, not usually interested in her movements. Do you understand?"

"Yes," Virginia said, wondering if anyone could understand such a garbled statement.

"Then that is very kind of you," the Duchess said. "Perhaps you would slip upstairs and put on your riding habit, and just ask one of the footmen to have a horse brought to the front door. You will have to hurry, although, of course, the pony-cart goes very slowly."

"Yes, Your Grace, I will go at once," Virginia said.

"Then here is the message," the Duchess said, drawing a small envelope from the waistband which encircled her small waist. "There will be no need for you to wait after you have given it to Miss Marshbanks. She will understand."

"Very well," Virginia said.

She took the envelope and turned towards the door.

"Hurry!" the Duchess said impatiently. "Please hurry, Miss Langholme! There is no time to be lost."

Virginia obeyed her and ran into the hall. There was a footman on duty near the front door.

"Will you ask the grooms to bring me round a horse immediately?" she said. "The mare I rode yesterday will do."

"Yes, miss," the footman replied.

Virginia ran up the stairs. It only took her a few minutes to change into her riding things. By the time she was down again the horse was already at the door.

"Would you like a groom to go with you, miss?" asked the man who was holding the bridle.

"No," Virginia answered. "I am only going a short distance."

"Very good, miss."

She cantered off down the drive. She knew where the village lay; for they had passed through it on her arrival at the Castle and, indeed, it was less than a mile beyond the park gates. As soon as she was out of sight of the Castle she flicked her horse with the whip and he sprang into a gallop. Nevertheless, when she passed through the drive gates there was no sign of Miss Marshbanks in the pony-cart.

The road outside the Castle was not a main one and she could ride at quite a good pace, keeping to the grass verges. She reached the village in a very few minutes. There was a village green with a duck-pond, a grey stone church dating from Norman times, a public house called The Nag's Head, the village stocks, empty but somehow menacing, and tucked away amongst some small, half-timbered houses she saw the post office and outside it the pony-cart.

It took her only a few seconds to gallop across the green to the post office. She dismounted and seeing two small boys holding the head of the fat, slow pony which Miss Marshbanks drove, she told one of them to come to the head of her own horse.

"Hold him gently," she said, "but do not let him go."

"Oi wonna't do that, ma'am," the boy said in broad, country accents.

Virginia ran into the post office. Miss Marshbanks was standing at the counter writing something.

"Oh, Miss Marshbanks!" Virginia said breathlessly.

Miss Marshbanks turned to look at her with an almost comical expression of surprise.

"Miss Langholme! What on earth do you want?" she asked, and as she spoke she covered with her hand the piece of paper on which she was writing.

"The Duchess sent me," Virginia answered. "She asked me to give you this note."

She drew the envelope, as she spoke, from the fringed pocket of her suède bolero into which she had slipped it. Miss Marshbanks opened it and read the contents.

"Oh, I understand!" she said. "Thank you very much, Miss Langholme. It was very kind of you to get here so quickly. In fact, you were just in time."

In taking the Duchess's message from Virginia, Miss Marshbanks had raised her hand, and Virginia saw it had covered a telegram form.

"The Duchess was afraid I should not be in time to stop you doing whatever you were about to do," Virginia said.

Once again Miss Marshbanks covered the telegram in front of her.

"I hope your horse is all right, Miss Langholme," she said meaningly.

Virginia smiled.

"I will go and see," she said.

She went outside to find her horse was quite quiet as the small boy was feeding the mare with an apple. As Virginia reached his side she realised she had no money with her and she turned and went back into the post office.

"I am sorry, Miss Marshbanks . . ." she said.

Miss Marshbanks was just in the process of handing over the telegram to the Postmaster behind the counter.

"Well, what is it, Miss Langholme?" she asked, and this time her voice was querulous.

"I am so sorry to bother you again," Virginia said, "but I came away in such a hurry that I have no money. I should like to reward the boy who looked after my horse."

"Oh, of course!" Miss Marshbanks said, her tone changing. She opened her handbag and took out a silver sixpence. "I am afraid it is rather a lot," she said apologetically, "but as we come from the Castle we do not want them to talk."

"No, of course not," Virginia said, wondering why they should talk and why it mattered anyway.

She went out of the post office and gave the boy the sixpence. He was overjoyed. He pulled his forelock several times and rubbed the sixpence against his ragged jacket.

"Oi'll 'old yer 'orse any time yer comes 'ere, ma'am," he said.

Virginia laughed.

"I am afraid you are not going to make a fortune out of me," she replied, and swinging herself into the saddle rode off.

She went back more slowly, enjoying the quiet, English road with its high hedges of honeysuckle and flowering briars, and the sunshine which, now the sun had risen, was warm on her face. She turned in at the great gates. She had glanced at them on her arrival but now their intricate ironwork, tipped with gold, and the stone lions supporting the family crest, on pillars on either side, filled her with delight. It was exactly what she thought the gateway to a great house should look like.

"I believe I am really a snob," she told herself as she cantered gently down the drive. "I thought I should hate the ostentation of England. Instead of which, it is all in such beautiful taste, nothing jars, nothing offends." Then she thought of Marcus Ryll and added: "Except, of course, some of the people."

She drew her horse in to a walk and was moving quietly under the trees when she saw the Duke riding towards her. She felt her heart turn over in her breast and knew that in future this feeling, as if the world rocked beneath her and her breathing was suddenly constricted, would always happen whenever she saw him. She drew her horse to a standstill and waited, her eyes shining, her face radiant as he came towards her.

"Virginia!" he exclaimed, and she saw he had been riding hard and long, for his horse was sweating. "I have been thinking," he said, "and I think best when I am travelling fast."

She did not answer him because somehow there was no need for words. They had but to be together, they had only to look into each other's eyes, to know that nothing else in the world mattered. The two horses moved side by side up the drive.

"Where have you been?" the Duke asked.

Virginia parted her lips to tell him and then she remembered what the Duchess had said. She had no wish to deceive the man she loved, and yet, as the Duchess had asked her for secrecy, it seemed hardly right to betray her trust.

"I have been riding," she answered truthfully.

"Did I ever tell you how lovely you look on a horse?" he asked.

"I am beginning to get conceited," Virginia smiled.

"Shall I really tell you what I think about you?" he asked, but she shook her head.

"We are in sight of the Castle," she reminded him. "We must not be suspected; indeed, we must be very careful."

She thought how Lady Shelmadine had tried to enslave the Duke and knew her for a bitter enemy.

"You are shivering," the Duke said. "What is it?"

"I think I am afraid," Virginia replied. "In fact, I know I am. I am afraid not only for your life but because we are happy. Nothing escapes . . . some people."

Instinctively the Duke glanced towards the Castle and the expression of love was wiped from his face.

"You are right, Virginia," he said. "We must be careful."

"Lady . . . Lady Shelmadine . . ." Virginia stammered.

"I know," he answered, "but I did not realise that you knew that too."

"Women are perceptive," Virginia said.

"I understand," he answered. "I am being a fool. Forgive me, Virginia, if you can."

He turned his horse and, as if he had met her casually, raised his hat and left her, riding towards the stables. Automatically Virginia turned her horse in the other direction, riding along the other side of the lake, until a quarter of an hour later she turned and came back through the trees in the park.

She went to the stables, left her horse and walked back to the Castle. She entered the hall, feeling as if the whole atmosphere had changed. Before it had seemed warm and somehow secure. Now there was a feeling of treachery and of danger about it.

She walked slowly up the staircase towards her bedroom. As she reached the top stair she looked back and saw Lady Shelmadine coming from the library. She was frowning and there was an expression of anger on her lovely face. Virginia felt her heart contract. Was she being stupid, or had Lady Shelmadine gone to the library in search of her? And, if so, what added trouble was there afoot?

9

VIRGINIA overslept! She did not hear the well-trained maid come into the room to draw back the curtains and bring in the early morning tea. The small tray bore a tea-set of elegantly flowered china and two wafer-thin slices of bread-and-butter on a plate.

She came back to consciousness with a start and instinctively her hand went beneath her pillow to find the letter that rested there—the letter she had read not once but a dozen times the night before. Her first love-letter!

She sat up in bed now, her hair falling over her shoulders, her eyes shining, to open the thick, expensive writing-paper embossed with the Ducal crest. She already knew by heart what the letter contained and yet she read the words again.

My Mother and I have been asked to Chard this evening by the Duchess of Witherington to meet Their Majesties the King and Queen. I wish, above all things, that I need not go because all day I have been thinking that we might meet in our own special place beside the lake. But you will understand that this is an invitation that I cannot refuse and so I shall not see you.

Please stay in the house and do not walk about the grounds alone. I shall be thinking of you, and if you only knew how slowly the hours will pass!

There was no beginning nor end to the letter but Virginia thought, although she had never seen it before, that she would have recognised the strong, upright writing as belonging to the Duke.

She sat for a long time staring at the letter and then, almost without realising what she was doing, she lay down again on the pillow, going over that moment, as she had done a thousand times already, when he had held her in his arms and they had clung together like two frightened children. She had felt his heart beating, she had known the wonder of his lips. She felt the thrill of it make her quiver . . . Then she shivered!

At least last night he had been safe! She had heard the voices of the other guests in the house, when she walked down the passage past the dining-room. She had wondered then if Marcus and Lady Shelmadine would seize the opportunity after dinner to meet. Perhaps they had been surprised that one of the pills had not already worked and that the Duke was still alive. If that was so, then they would have conspired together how best to use the other three.

One day had passed. There were still six days left in which Marcus Ryll would try to destroy the Duke, because only in that way could he save himself from prison!

With a little feeling of exasperation Virginia wondered why, to save all this, the Duke did not give his cousin what he wanted. What did it matter that he would go on asking in future? At least for the moment the danger would be averted and it was nonsense for the Duke to say he could not afford it. The whole Castle was filled with treasures of every sort and description and, besides . . . Virginia gave a little sigh. She could not escape from that unemotional, matter of fact part of her which declared that there were millions of American dollars at the Duke's disposal should he care to use them.

She wondered what would happen if she wrote a cheque for the amount that Marcus Ryll required and sent it to him. Then she knew that it would be impossible for her to do such a thing without disclosing her own identity. No, she must trust the Duke to find a solution—and not one that he was rushed into by panic.

At the same time in her love for him she was horribly afraid. In all her life, in a country that was supposed to be rough and at times violent, she had never come up against murder or violence of any sort. Now that she was face to face with it, the stark horror of it made her tremble. It was worse, she thought, because it did not involve noise and anger or men impelled by their passions to strike at each other. It was cold and calculated, and sinister because, in its way, it was so civilised.

"Oh, Sebastian, be careful!" she whispered and realised that for the first time, even to herself, she had called him by his Christian name.

She suddenly became aware of the time. She jumped out of bed. It did not take her long to dress. Nevertheless the hands of the grandfather clock seemed accusing as she hurried down the staircase towards Miss Marshbanks' sitting-room.

She opened the door and hurried in with words of apology on her lips, only to find the room was empty. She saw at once that Miss Marshbanks had not yet had her breakfast.

"So she is late, too," Virginia thought with a little smile. She looked at the half a dozen covered, silver dishes arranged on a sidetable, on a silver hot-plate heated by six short candles in silver containers which could be snuffed out by turning a tiny handle. There were two different sorts of egg dishes, kedgeree, two sorts of fish and some grilled game.

Virginia wondered who ate the remains of all these vast meals; for she had already learned that, whilst she and Miss Marshbanks had the choice of five or six dishes, there were always at least a dozen in the dining-room, besides a cold collation of ham, brawn, pork, boar's head and other cold meats, which came in once and were never seen again.

Almost ashamed at not feeling hungry in the face of such munificent hospitality, Virginia helped herself sparingly to a little fish, and she was just pouring herself a cup of China tea when Miss Marshbanks came hurrying into the room.

"Good morning, Miss Langholme!" she said. "I am late because I thought that tiresome postman would never get here! Always the same excuse—the train was late! If you ask me, I think the delay is in the post office!"

Miss Marshbanks put a letter face-downwards on the table just inside the door, took off her hat and veil and placed them down on a chair. She glanced at the clock as she did so.

"I cannot go up to the Duchess now," she said, almost as if she were speaking to herself. "The pony-cart will be round in another ten minutes."

"Have you got to drive to the village this morning?" Virginia asked.

"Yes, the Duchess has asked me to take a message for her," Miss Marshbanks replied. Her lips tightened a little and there was something in her voice which told Virginia this was a forbidden subject and it would be unwise to question her further.

"Why did you have to meet the postman?" she asked. "Surely he was on his way to the Castle?"

Again she realised she had made a mistake. Miss Marshbanks frowned as she moved to the sidetable and there was an obvious pause before she said:

"Is the fish good? I am not very fond of fish dishes, they do not always suit me."

"Yes, very good," Virginia answered.

She wondered why there must be all this secrecy. It was so uncharacteristic of Miss Marshbanks to be reserved, to refuse to answer a question. As a general rule she was garrulous to the point of boredom and appeared only too willing to talk of everything and everybody.

Feeling a little uncomfortable because she had asked questions Virginia said:

"I am afraid I also was late! I overslept."

"There is no excuse for you," Miss Marshbanks smiled. "You did not go to the party last night."

There was an eager note in her voice which told Virginia she was forgiven. Miss Marshbanks had had a great deal to say the night before about the Duchess's friendship with the new King and Queen.

"Did Her Grace enjoy the party?" Virginia inquired.

"I saw her only for a moment this morning," Miss Marshbanks said. "She just had time to tell me that Her Majesty was lovelier than ever and His Majesty in splendid form. They are coming to Ryll as soon as the shooting starts. His Grace will have to start making plans quite soon, if it is to be a party on the scale that their Majesties will expect at Ryll."

"What do they shoot?" Virginia asked.

"Pheasants," Miss Marshbanks replied. "The last time the King was here—of course he was the Prince of Wales then—the bag was over two thousand brace. There was a dinner-party for sixty in the evening and a dance the following night. I can tell you, I was worked off my feet."

"I am sure you were," Virginia sympathised.

She felt, suddenly, as if someone had put a heavy hand

upon her heart. So the Duke was arranging Royal parties two or three months ahead—and she would not be here! It seemed to her as if the sunlight outside was somehow dimmed. Whatever the dangers, she felt certain that the Duke would in some miraculous way or other surmount them, but her own problems would remain unsolved.

Miss Marshbanks poured herself another cup of strong, Indian tea.

"I must go," she said almost mechanically. "There never seems to be time for everything in this house. If the Duchess asks for me by any chance, please tell her I shall not be long and that the letter she was expecting has arrived. She will understand."

Miss Marshbanks jumped up from the table and picking up her hat from where she had laid it on the chair by the door, put it on her head and secured it to her hair with a long hat-pin ornamented at the end by a little clump of jet beads. Her veil was spotted and, Virginia thought, unbecoming, but Miss Marshbanks tied it skilfully over her face and tucked the ends out of sight under the ribbons which trimmed her plain straw hat.

"I shall not be long," she said again with a smile and went from the room.

Virginia looked out of the window. She wondered where the Duke was. Maybe he was tired from the night before but she doubted it. She longed to go riding, perhaps in search of him, but she thought that to do so might seem strange and rather presumptuous. Yesterday the Duchess had told her to ride, but no one had invited her to do so today and she felt shy of ordering a horse to be brought round.

She supposed that she must work, though now her pretence of studying books in the library seemed a farce. All she wanted was to be with the Duke; she admitted to herself that she longed to see him, that her whole body ached to be beside him.

She rose from the breakfast-table and, resisting an impulse to go out into the sunshine, walked down the passage and across the hall to the library. There was no one about. She assumed that the other guests in the house rose late, breakfasting either in their bedrooms or in the *boudoirs* adjoining them.

Virginia wondered if Lady Shelmadine had passed a good night. Had she lain worrying whether her nefarious plan would succeed? Or had she, perhaps, seized the opportunity to be with her lover? Virginia felt herself shudder. It was all rather horrible and she went into the library slamming the door behind her.

With an effort she forced herself to read one of the many books on the family history, but it all reminded her too vividly of the Duke. His face seemed to leap out at her from the old prints. She found that every time she came to his Christian name, which was a family one, or even his title, she could think only of him.

She must have been reading for nearly an hour when the door of the library opened and the Duchess appeared. She was very elegantly dressed in one of her dove-grey morning gowns with a huge bunch of Parma violets nestling amongst the chiffon which trimmed the bodice, but her face looked tired and her voice was petulant as she asked:

"Are you there, Miss Langholme? I wondered if you had seen Miss Marshbanks?"

Virginia put down the book she was reading and rose to her feet.

"Good morning, Your Grace! Miss Marshbanks has gone to the village in the pony-cart. She said she had something to do for you."

"Oh, yes, of course!" the Duchess said. "I had forgotten. But surely she should be back by now. I cannot think why she did not come to see me before she left."

"She asked me to tell you, if you asked, that she would not be long," Virginia said, "and that the letter you were expecting had arrived."

"It has!" the Duchess's face lit up, her voice lost its querulousness and sounded excited. "Oh, why did she not bring it to me?"

"The postman was late," Virginia explained. "Miss Marshbanks only had time to snatch her breakfast and set off for the village."

"Oh, well, that explains it," the Duchess said. "What has she done with the letter?"

"I think it is in her sitting-room," Virginia replied. "Shall I fetch it for you?"

"That would be very kind," the Duchess said.

"I will not be a minute," Virginia promised.

"No, wait! I will come with you," the Duchess said. As she spoke she glanced over her shoulder. "One never knows who might be about."

Virginia did not reply. They walked together down the passage, the Duchess's silken petticoats making a soft hissing sound as she moved, the train of her dress trailing on the carpets. Virginia had the feeling they were hurrying, as if the Duchess was eager to reach the letter. She remembered the letter that the Duchess had pounced on in the Duke's folder two days ago and she guessed that this letter was from the same source.

They reached the sitting-room. The letter was where Miss Marshbanks had left it on the table, face-downwards.

"I think this is what you are looking for," Virginia said.

The Duchess picked up the letter with fingers which suddenly looked greedy and almost like claws.

"Yes, that is it!" she exclaimed in tones of triumph. "Well, Sebastian certainly will not keep it from me this month."

She turned and went from the room without another word. Virginia stood staring after her. There was something spiteful in the way the Duchess had said that Sebastian would not keep it from her, and now Virginia wondered if she had been wise to give her the letter in Miss Marshbank's absence.

Almost apprehensively she went to the window and looked out. She could see quite a long stretch of the drive beyond the bridge where it crossed the lake. There was no sign of the pony-cart.

"I do not suppose she will be long," Virginia said to herself, but somehow she felt unhappy.

She walked down the passage and back to the hall. There was no sign of the Duchess. The waiting footman opened the front door and she stood on the grey stone steps looking out over the sunlit parkland. The lake, like a silver mirror, held the reflections of the black and white swans. It was all very serene and peaceful.

Then under the trees nearly a mile away Virginia saw the pony-cart. There was no mistaking Miss Marshbanks' straw hat as she sat, bolt upright, holding the reins. The pony was quiet and fat and did not hurry.

It took over ten minutes for the pony-cart to come down the drive, over the bridge and on to the big, gravel sweep in front of the Castle. As it reached the front door a groom came running from the stables to take the pony's head.

"Will you be wanting the pony any more today, miss?" Virginia heard him ask respectfully.

"No, I do not think so, Jed," Miss Marshbanks replied. "If I do I will let you know. He was very good today and did not shy even when a piece of paper blew across the road in front of him."

" 'E be getting lazy, that's what wrong with 'im, miss," the groom said with a grin.

Miss Marshbanks stepped out of the cart. She shut the door behind her and turned to climb the steps to the front door. Then she saw Virginia waiting.

"Hello, Miss Langholme!" she exclaimed. "Are you waiting for me?"

"Yes, I am," Virginia replied. "I have something to tell you."

Even as she spoke she realised that Matthews had appeared behind her and checked what she had been going to say.

"Forgive me, miss," the butler said to Miss Marshbanks, "but her Grace has been asking for you for over half an hour. She will be obliged if you will go to her immediately."

"Yes, of course," Miss Marshbanks replied. "I will see you later, Miss Langholme."

She swept into the hall before Virginia could say anything further and hurried up the stairs towards the Duchess's *boudoir*. Virginia gave a little sigh of relief. There had been nothing to worry about. The Duchess was just impatient. She walked towards the library. She had just reached it when she heard a voice calling her.

"Miss Langholme! Miss Langholme!"

She turned and hurried back. Leaning over the balustrade at the top of the staircase Miss Marshbanks was shouting her name.

"Yes, I am here," Virginia replied.

"Will you come upstairs?" Miss Marshbanks asked.

There was something in her tone which made Virginia run. She picked up her dress and hurried up the staircase to arrive, a little breathless, where Miss Marshbanks stood at the top.

"You were going to tell me something," Miss Marshbanks said. "What was it?"

"I was only going to tell you that the Duchess wanted you," Virginia said.

"You have seen her! What did she say?" Miss Marshbanks inquired.

"She came to the library," Virginia said, "and I gave her the message that you would not be long and that the letter had come."

"What happened then?" Miss Marshbanks interposed.

"She asked for the letter," Virginia replied, "and we walked to the sitting-room because I knew where you had left it."

"You gave it to her!" Miss Marshbanks exclaimed.

"She wanted it," Virginia answered. "Was that wrong? I felt perhaps she should have waited."

"If she has taken it herself . . . Oh, she cannot . . ." Miss Marshbanks' voice was suddenly full of fear.

She met Virginia's eyes and as if they both simultaneously had the same thought they turned and hurried down the long corridor. It took them some time to reach the part of the Castle where Lord Rufton had his rooms. The corridor turned and twisted and then, suddenly, they saw ahead Mr. Warner in his white coat standing outside the door.

Miss Marshbanks reached his side, breathlessly, her hat a little awry from the speed at which she had hurried.

"Good morning . . . Mr. Warner!" she gasped, "have . . . you seen . . . Her . . . Grace?"

"Good morning, Miss Marshbanks!" Mr. Warner replied. "Yes, indeed. Her Grace is with his Lordship."

"Alone?"

Mr. Warner looked uncomfortable.

"Her Grace insisted, Miss Marshbanks. I knew it was not usual but she told me to wait outside and, really, what could I do?"

Miss Marshbanks thrust him on one side.

"She should not be there alone," she said. She moved towards the door. It was only when her hand was actually on the handle that she paused a moment and almost instinctively straightened her hat. Then she opened the door.

For a moment Virginia could see nothing because Miss Marshbanks was in front of her. Then she heard a sudden cry, not unlike that of an animal in pain, as Miss Marshbanks rushed forward. The Duchess was seated at the desk but her arms were sprawled over it and the ink-pot had fallen on to the floor, its contents spilled on to the carpet. Standing above her was Lord Rufton with both hands round her throat!

"Stop him! Stop him!" Miss Marshbanks screamed, and with a bound Mr. Warner had reached Lord Rufton's side and was pulling away the old man's hands.

He released the Duchess and as Virginia watched, too

horrified to move or make a sound, the Duchess fell from the desk and toppled sideways in a crumpled heap on to the floor beside it.

"Your Grace! Oh, my God! Your Grace!" Miss Marshbanks was screaming as she knelt beside the Duchess, rubbing her hands.

Virginia could see that the Duchess's habitually white face was now crimson, her eyes seeming to protrude from their sockets, her mouth gaping open.

"Water! Get ... water ... brandy ... anything!" Miss Marshbanks screamed, and as Virginia turned to obey a voice from the doorway demanded:

"What is going on here?"

"Sebastian!" She breathed the name rather than spoke it and turned to him with a sense of utter relief.

The Duke took in at a glance Mr. Warner trying to settle the restless old Lord Rufton in a chair and Miss Marshbanks screaming beside the Duchess's body on the floor.

"What has he done to her? Oh, Your Grace, what has he done to her?" Miss Marshbanks cried at the sight of him.

The Duke stepped forward, bent down and picked up his mother in his arms.

"Come with me, both of you!" he said sharply, and walked through the open door and down the corridor.

He moved swiftly and Miss Marshbanks followed him, sobbing as she went. Virginia came behind, shocked by what she had seen and feeling as if she moved in some strange and horrible nightmare from which she could not awake. It seemed a very long way to the Duchess's room. The Duke waited a moment for Miss Marshbanks to open the door and then carried his mother inside and set her down on the great, canopied bed, which stood on a platform, covered with white fur rugs.

"Brandy!" he said sharply.

Miss Marshbanks ran to the wash-hand stand. On the marble top was a small, cut-glass decanter which was obviously familiar to her. She drew out the stopper and poured out some of the brandy into a tooth-glass; then the Duke, with his arm around his mother's shoulders, propped her up on the bed and held the glass to her lips.

Virginia could see that her eyes no longer protruded and that some of the ghastly colour had gone from her face.

"She is still alive," Miss Marshbanks whispered.

The Duke tried to force some of the brandy between his mother's lips. It seemed as if he succeeded for after a moment the Duchess's eyes flickered.

"She is alive," Miss Marshbanks said again. "Oh, praise be to God, she is alive!"

The Duchess's lips moved as if she would have spoken and then, suddenly, her whole body seemed seized by a convulsion which shook her all over; her head fell back and she was still. Very gently the Duke set her down against the pillow.

Miss Marshbanks gave a heart-rending cry.

"She is dead! Oh, Your Grace, do something! She must not die. She cannot die . . . like this!"

The Duke stood looking down at his mother, and for a moment Virginia, watching him, thought that he had not heard Miss Marshbanks. Then he said quietly:

"Yes, she is dead!"

He walked across the room and closed the door which was half-open from their entrance.

"Listen, both of you," he said. "I have something to say. Listen, Miss Marshbanks, this is important!"

His voice was suddenly sharp and Miss Marshbanks, who had seemed on the verge of collapse, appeared to pull herself together.

"Yes, Your Grace," she murmured.

"My mother is dead," the Duke said slowly as if he chose his words, "and she has died from a heart attack. As you know, Miss Marshbanks, her heart has been troubling her for some years and the doctor has been called to her on several occasions. I am going to send for him now and you will neither of you—do you understand this? neither of you—mention to him, or to anyone else, what has just occurred in Lord Rufton's rooms. I will have no scandal in this family! You know, as well as I do, that a report that my mother had been throttled to death by a guest in the Castle—a man who when he was young was extremely distinguished—would bring most unwelcome publicity to our family. That I would never countenance."

The Duke drew a deep breath. He had seemed to be speaking directly to Miss Marshbanks, but for a moment his eyes flickered over Virginia.

"As I have already said," he went on, "there must be no scandal and you, Miss Marshbanks, will appreciate that it is the one thing my mother would have disliked as much as

I should dislike and deprecate it. We will, therefore, make quite certain that nothing is known by anyone of this incredible incident."

"Mr. Warner . . . knows what . . . happened," Miss Marshbanks murmured, her voice choked by sobs.

"I will deal with Mr. Warner," the Duke said sternly. "He should never have permitted Her Grace to break the very stringent rule I had made that no one should enter Lord Rufton's rooms alone. I have known for a long time that Lord Rufton is suffering from a disease of the brain which often causes its sufferers to attack those of whom they are most fond. That is why I always insisted, Miss Marshbanks, that you, or someone else, should accompany my mother when she visited her old friend. My orders have been disobeyed."

"It was not my fault, Your Grace. I had been to the village."

"On what errand?" the Duke asked sternly.

To Virginia's surprise Miss Marshbanks merely dropped her head and did not reply.

"You see, Miss Marshbanks, you are in part to blame for what has occurred," the Duke said.

"Oh, I know! I know!" Miss Marshbanks sobbed. "Oh, Your Grace, how can I ever forgive myself?"

"You can at least make sure that there will be no talk about the way in which my mother has died," the Duke said. "I would ask you, Miss Marshbanks, because I know you loved my mother, to accord her one last service. I should like you to undress her and put her into her nightgown. Place around her neck the pearl and diamond collar that she so often wore."

Miss Marshbanks hesitated a moment; then going to the Duchess's dressing-table and taking a small key from a mother-of-pearl and diamond box, she opened with it one of the drawers. Virginia saw that the drawer contained a number of velvet covered jewellery boxes. Miss Marshbanks drew one out. She opened it and there lay a magnificent collar of pearls such as, Virginia knew, many women who had long necks affected in the evening. It comprised five rows of pearls intersected with long, diamond bars which held the collar upright.

"Yes, that is the one," the Duke said. "Place it around my mother's neck, Miss Marshbanks, and I will give orders that it is not to be removed since she wished to be buried in it. When the doctor comes, try to arrange that there is also a scarf over her shoulders. He will be listening for her heart, for he will have expected her to die of a heart attack—and that, indeed, is the truth. She was alive when I carried her from Lord Rufton's rooms and, as you both saw, the experience she suffered affected her heart. She did not, in actual fact, die of strangulation, she died of a heart attack. Is that clear?"

"Yes, indeed," Miss Marshbanks said.

"And you, Miss Langholme! You also understand?" the Duke said. "You are a newcomer to our midst, but I feel that you understand this is a matter of family pride, of family honour, and I would ask you for your word that nothing you have seen shall be repeated outside this room."

"You have my word," Virginia said quietly.

The Duke walked to the bed and stood looking down at the Duchess. As if this moment between mother and son was something on which no one should intrude, Virginia turned away. Miss Marshbanks had already crossed the room and was pulling down the blinds.

Then the Duke said, and his voice seemed to break a silence which had become almost oppressive:

"I am going to send for the doctor. You, Miss Marshbanks, will do what I have asked of you. And you, Miss Langholme, will please stand outside the door to prevent anyone from entering. I do not wish my mother's lady's-maid, or anyone else, to know that she is dead until Miss Marshbanks is ready to show her to the doctor."

"I understand," Virginia said in a voice that seemed suddenly caught in her throat.

The Duke turned and left the room. Virginia looked at Miss Marshbanks, who now, once again, stood at the bedside, her face convulsed with tears.

"Is there anything I can do?" she asked.

"Only what . . . His Grace ordered," Miss Marshbanks said. "Oh, my p . . . poor . . . lady! That . . . this should have . . . happened to her."

"You must not blame yourself," Virginia said.

"If only I . . . had not . . . left the . . . letter behind!" Miss Marshbanks said with a cry of despair.

Virginia wanted to comfort her, but she knew that now was not the moment. There was something they both had to do; so she went from the room, closing the door behind her, and stood in the corridor outside. The Duchess's room was, fortunately, at the far end of the landing, and as the housemaids had finished their rooms there was no one about.

Virginia stood for a little while; then feeling as if her legs could no longer support her she sat down on one of the velvet-covered, high-backed chairs which stood at intervals along the corridor.

Now, at last, the full significance of what had happened began to creep over her. She thought she would never forget that moment when she had seen Lord Rufton, with an almost diabolical expression on his face, gripping the Duchess by the throat. Then, as the picture of what she had seen came back to her—the Duchess's limp, outstretched hands with their glittering rings, her face, crimson and convulsed with its staring eyes, the ink-pot upset over the carpet and the quill pen lying beside it—she remembered something else.

On the floor, as if it, too, had been pushed from the desk, was lying a piece of paper, the same size, shape and colour as that which the Duchess had asked Lord Rufton to sign when she had taken Virginia with her to visit him. She had said, then, it was a love-letter which he had written to her years earlier. But even in the horror and confusion of the Duchess slipping, strangled, from the desk, Virginia had seen the piece of paper and realised now without any shadow of a doubt that it was a cheque-form!

10

THE Castle was very quiet. It seemed to Virginia that everyone had gone to the funeral except herself. The Duke had insisted that it should be private and that only members of the family and household should be present. Even so, there had been an enormous crowd of people to follow the coffin, covered in white lilies, which was carried by the gardeners and foresters from the Castle to the family vault in the chapel in the park.

From behind a drawn blind Virginia watched them winding their way like a long, dark crocodile, in the warm sunshine which was at variance with the black garments and crape veils.

The last three days had been a nightmare for Miss Marshbanks and yet, although many of the arrangements for the funeral fell on her shoulders, Virginia was aware that having so much to do had sustained her and kept her from collapse.

Virginia learned that many of the relations resented the Duke's instructions to have the funeral so quickly. They had been incensed, also, at his insisting that the coffin should be closed down so that the Duchess's body could not be seen by those who wished to pay their last respects.

Only Miss Marshbanks and Virginia had known why this was imperative; only they had been aware that the discoloration which had taken place could not be wholly attributed to a heart attack.

Because Miss Marshbanks had no one else in whom to confide, Virginia had to hear it all. How the women from the estate who had come to lay out the Duchess, as was traditional, had been offended by Miss Marshbanks' presence in the bedroom; how they complained that the drawn blinds made it hard for them to do their work; and how they had been curious at the Duke's command that his mother should be buried with her pearl and diamond collar round her neck.

"They were not likely to argue with His Grace, of course," Miss Marshbanks said, "only I got the brunt of it!"

"But now," Virginia thought, with a little sigh of relief, "the ordeal was nearly over." Yesterday Lord Rufton had been taken away by two male nurses in a closed carriage. Tonight, or at the latest first thing tomorrow morning, everyone staying in the Castle would leave, either by carriage or by train.

Virginia had been glad to learn that Lady Shelmadine would go too, but she knew that did not mean defeat or that she had given up plotting and planning the destruction of the Duke with Marcus Ryll. The only reason she was leaving was that without a chaperon it was impossible for her to stay on in the Castle.

Virginia had encountered Lady Shelmadine immediately after the Duchess's death, and if it had not been so frightening she would have been amused by what happened. The doctor had arrived, and Virginia, knowing that her position as watchdog at the Duchess's door was no longer necessary, had moved down the corridor and realised, when she reached the top of the stairs, that the Duke had already told the household of his mother's death.

The blinds were drawn and the Great Hall was almost in darkness. Then, as Virginia descended the stairs, Lady

Shelmadine came in through the front door. Obviously she had been out walking. She stood for a moment looking around her, then, lifting her skirt, she started to hurry up the stairs. Half-way up she came face to face with Virginia.

"Oh, Miss Langholme!" she exclaimed. "I did not see you. It is so dark! The blinds are drawn. Can it be that someone is dead?"

Virginia saw the sudden glint of excitement in Lady Shelmadine's eyes and after pausing a moment she said quietly:

"Yes, I have very bad news. Someone is dead!"

"Oh, it cannot be!" Lady Shelmadine cried. "Poor Sebastian! How terrible! What has occurred?"

Virginia did not answer at once. Then, as Lady Shelmadine looked inquiringly up into her face, she asked:

"But why should you assume that anything has happened to the Duke? His Grace is in excellent health. It is the Duchess who has died . . . !"

If she had not been so terrified for the Duke's life she would have laughed at the emotion which convulsed Lady Shelmadine's face. She knew, then, exactly what the woman was feeling—at first, disappointment that her evil plotting with Marcus Ryll had not materialised, and, secondly, the sudden fear that their poison had, in fact, killed the wrong person.

"The D . . . Duchess!" Lady Shelmadine managed to stutter.

"Yes, the Duchess," Virginia repeated. "A very strange and sudden attack. The doctor will, perhaps, be able to explain how it had happened."

As she turned and walked downstairs leaving Lady Shelmadine standing indecisively on the staircase, she hoped, but almost against hope, that she had frightened her. She knew, however, that time was passing and that Marcus Ryll would fight like a cornered rat rather than face bankruptcy and prison.

It was impossible for Virginia to see the Duke alone. Sometimes, walking along the passages, she had a glimpse of him moving amongst his relations or giving orders to the servants, but it seemed at times as if he had forgotten her very existence.

She supposed that she should go away, and it would, of course, have been the right and tactful thing to do. But she knew that nothing save a direct command from the Duke himself would force her to leave the Castle until she knew that he was safe. And, what was more, she thought with a little wry smile, she was of no social consequence. Miss Marshbanks would be considered sufficient chaperon as far as she was concerned, whilst Lady Shelmadine lived on a different level of the social structure.

There were three days left in which Marcus Ryll must make his move or fail in his attempt to destroy the Duke. Virginia was sure that by now he and Lady Shelmadine would have used up all the pills. They would therefore have to try some other method; apart from which, it would have looked strange if both the Duchess and Duke should die of a heart attack so close to each other.

What action, then, could Marcus take? Virginia racked her brains. He would not dare to shoot the Duke. That would obviously involve him in a charge of murder. He could drown him, but the Duke was not likely to go swimming in the lake. What weapon, then, would he choose?

Virginia suddenly felt as if the Castle, with its sightless windows, its darkened rooms and atmosphere of death, was suffocating her. She knew she must get outside in the sunshine. She must get away from the fear which haunted her every moment and try to think clearly. There would be no one to see her in the grounds; so she went from her room as she was, without putting on a hat.

As Virginia moved along the darkened corridor she knew she was desperately afraid of what would happen when the mourners who had filled the Castle departed. If only the Duke would leave too. If only she could take him away to California, to Virginia, to Texas—anywhere where he would be safe from the machinations of evil. The idea came to her like a ray of light, but she knew at once the Duke would never run away. It was not part of his character—and yet if only she could persuade him!

Virginia reached the top of the stairs and looked down into the empty marble hall. As she did so she saw a woman move against the dark panelling. At first she thought it must be someone who had not, after all, gone to the funeral. Then she realised that the woman she saw was in white and a moment later there was no one there. She held on to the top of the banisters, feeling suddenly faint.

"I imagined it," she told herself fiercely. "It was just a trick of the light." But she knew, even as she protested and argued with herself, that she had seen the White Lady. She had been there—a woman in white, moving through the hall, and then there was nothing!

"I dreamed it! It was just a figment of my imagination!" Virginia whispered. She told herself the ghost had appeared because of the Duchess, but she knew that explanation was not valid. It was before a member of the family died that the ghost appeared, and she knew by now that a member of the family meant, in actual fact, someone of the Ryll blood. The Duchess was a Ryll only by marriage!

Virginia wanted to cry out in terror at her own thoughts. Then, as she stood there irresolute, she heard a little scream. It was unmistakably a human voice that made the sound and it came again, only a little fainter.

Instinctively Virginia walked along the passage. She knew now where the sound came from—Marcus Ryll's room, the room from which she had taken the poison which was to have destroyed the Duke. She reached the room, saw the door was ajar and pushed it open. Inside there were two people who appeared to be struggling with each other. Then, as they saw her, they started and fell apart, their expressions comical in their dismay.

Virginia recognised Mary, the little, apple-cheeked country maid who often waited on her. She was an attractive girl, and beside her was one of the footmen, a tall, good-looking, fair boy who, Virginia knew, was called James.

"I heard someone scream," Virginia said.

"Oh, miss! I'm sorry!" Mary replied. "I didn't know anyone was left in the Castle. You won't tell on me, miss? Please! If you do, Mrs. Stone will dismiss me without a reference. Oh, please, miss . . ."

"Do not worry," Virginia assured her. "I heard you scream and thought something must be wrong."

"No, indeed, miss," Mary explained. "It was just that James was teasing me with a sword. I know we shouldn't be larking about at such a moment and you must forgive us."

"A sword?" Virginia asked curiously.

"No, ma'am," James interposed, " 'tis not a sword, 'tis a sword-stick. I found it when I was a cleaning Captain Ryll's things and I thought I'd show it to Mary, but she screamed at the sight of it. And that's 'ow you 'eard us, ma'am."

"A sword-stick!" Virginia mused. "I do not think I have ever heard of such a thing."

"I'll show it to you, ma'am," James said eagerly. "That is, if you won't tell Captain Ryll that I showed it to you."

"No, I will not tell him," Virginia said.

The footman picked up the stick from the bed where he had thrown it, hastily, at Virginia's appearance. She saw it was a short swagger-cane such as officers in the Army carried. James twisted the band of gold which ornamented it, and it divided. Then he drew out from the bottom half a long, evil-looking, rapier-like sword. It was over two feet in length with a very sharp point.

" 'Tis what officers carry in the tropics, ma'am," James explained. "I've 'eard about such weapons but I've never seen one before, and I only found it when I was a polishing th' gold band. I felt it move and when I turned it round I understands why."

"Yes, I see," Virginia said.

" 'Tis as sharp as a razor at th' point," James went on. "You could kill a man with it easy."

Virginia took a deep breath.

"Thank you for showing it to me, James," she said, "but I think you should put it away. I should not mention your discovery to Captain Ryll."

"No, I shan't, ma'am. 'E's a strange gentleman to work for. I wouldn't like to be with 'im permanent."

"I am sure you would rather be with His Grace," Virginia said.

She turned to Mary, who was watching James with an expression approaching adoration in her eyes.

"They will soon be coming back from the funeral service," she said. "If I were you, Mary, I should return to your work."

"And you won't tell on us, will you, miss?" Mary asked anxiously.

"No, I promise," Virginia answered.

She walked away, feeling sick and frightened. Was the sword-stick a new threat to the Duke? Was that how Marcus Ryll was now determined to kill him? To stab him, perhaps, when he was alone in the garden. It seemed a dangerous method, but who could fathom the workings of a murderer's mind? She knew only one thing—that she must warn the Duke. He must know what fresh danger threatened him.

It was not easy to find a way to speak to the Duke, in fact it was quite impossible. Miss Marshbanks returned from the funeral in floods of tears, and it was Virginia who had to arrange the seating for dinner, check the arrangements for the departing guests and see that the menservants knew who were leaving that evening and who the following morning.

By the time Virginia had finished doing all the things that Miss Marshbanks should have done the Duke had gone upstairs to dress for dinner, and she thought despairingly that there would be no chance to see him alone; for on the previous night, and the night before, he had sat up until late with his relations.

She hoped against hope that he would somehow communicate with her, but when after dinner there was no message she knew that she must get in touch with him. She wrote him a little note saying that she must see him and wondered how best she could get it to him. Then she remembered the plans which the Duke had given her and which he had said were valuable. She went to the library and fetched them. She placed her note inside one of the maps, and carrying the folder in her hand she went in search of Matthews. She could not find him but she encountered James carrying a grog-tray into the salon.

"James," she said, "I want you to do something for me."

"Of course, ma'am," he answered.

"Then take this and put it on His Grace's dressing-table," she said. "Nowhere else! Do you understand? There is something very valuable in here that I would not wish left lying about and I should like His Grace to know it's in his safe keeping when he retires tonight."

"Very good, ma'am," James said.

Then Virginia hesitated.

"No, on second thoughts," she said, "I think His Grace would rather have it earlier. When he comes out of the dining-room do you think you could contrive to give it to him?"

"I'll manage it somehow, ma'am," James said stoutly.

"Thank you," Virginia said and slipped away for fear that someone should see her talking to James and ask the footman what she had said.

She went to the sitting-room and waited. Miss Marshbanks had refused any dinner and had gone to her room to sob convulsively on her bed. There was nothing Virginia could say or do to comfort her. She knew that now it was all over it was best for the poor woman to let herself go.

It was hard to sit in the small room and wait. But there

was nothing else Virginia could do and she thought that time had never passed so slowly. Ten o'clock came ... eleven o'clock ... and she thought, despairingly, that James must have failed to reach the Duke, when he suddenly appeared in the door, the silver salver in his hand.

" 'Is Grace's compliments, ma'am," he said, "and 'e asks that you'll put the plans away in his desk in the library. 'E says that you'll know where the key is kept."

"Oh, thank you, James," Virginia said. "Yes, I know where the key is kept."

She could hardly wait until James had shut the door before she opened the plans to find, as she had expected, a piece of paper inserted amongst them. There were only a few words scribbled on a bridge-scorer, but at least they told her what she wanted to know.

Meet me at five o'clock tomorrow morning in the stable-yard, he had written, and Virginia held it against her cheek before she went upstairs to her bedroom.

She was up long before five the next morning. When she left the Castle there was no one stirring, but the stable-yard seemed full of people. The Duke was waiting for her astride the black stallion he habitually rode and her own horse was beside him, being saddled by two grooms while several others appeared to be taking instructions from the Duke.

"Good morning, Miss Langholme," the Duke said, conventionally raising his hat. "I thought perhaps you would enjoy a gallop before starting your day's work."

"Yes, indeed, Your Grace," Virginia replied demurely.

A groom helped her to mount and as she did so the Duke's stallion began to rear and paw the ground with his hooves.

" 'E's fresh, Your Grace," the groom said. " 'E 'asn't 'ad enough exercise these last few days."

"Then I will take him up to the flats," the Duke replied. "He will not feel so frisky after a good gallop."

"That's what 'e needs, Your Grace," the groom agreed.

Virginia and the Duke moved off, keeping, she noted, out of sight of the Castle and leaving the stable yard by the northern gate. They cantered for a short distance, the Duke's horse being extremely skittish. Then at last he turned and smiled at her.

"We have escaped!" he said, and she smiled back, feeling as if they were, indeed, playing truant.

"I have missed you," he said in a low voice, and she felt

her heart turn over in her breast because of the look in his eyes.

"I could not see you before," he said. "You understood, didn't you?"

"Of course," she answered.

"They were all round me, full of curiosity and suspicion," he said. "If they had had even a sight of you I think they would have guessed."

"Guessed what?" Virginia asked.

"That I love you," he answered. "I have thought of you every moment, every second, and the only consolation I had was that I knew you were in the Castle, I knew you were near me. Even though we could not be together, that meant more than I can ever say."

"I have something to tell you," Virginia said.

The Duke made a gesture of impatience.

"Must we talk about anything but ourselves?" he protested. "It seems a century since I last saw you, Virginia. I want only to talk to you. I want, more than anything else in the world, to kiss you."

Virginia felt as if it was hard to breathe when he spoke like that, but because she loved him she had to tell him what she knew he must hear.

"Listen!" she said. "Captain Ryll has a sword-stick in his room. I have never seen one before but it is a horrible, dangerous weapon. I can only think of one reason why he should want to use it."

"Damn him!" the Duke exclaimed. "Must he always be behind us casting a shadow over our happiness? Forget him, Virginia. Forget him until we have to turn for home. Give me your hand."

He drew nearer to her, and holding her reins with one hand she drew off her glove and held the other out to him. She felt the strength and warmth of his fingers and a thrill ran through her. She felt as if she suddenly came alive and that the mere touch of him swept away all her fears, her worries—everything except the joy of being with him. He bent his head and kissed her fingers, but the stallion, shying at a leaf blowing across the path, swept them apart.

"Shall we give the horses their heads?" the Duke suggested. "Then perhaps they will allow us to talk to each other."

"Where are we going?" Virginia asked, realising they were in a part of the estate she had never been to before.

"Up to what is known as 'the flats'," the Duke said. "It

is a wonderful place for a gallop and no one will see us."

He spurred his horse on and very shortly they left the low parkland and came to a wild strip of open country rising upwards towards the horizon. There, with the wind on their faces and the thunder of their horses' hooves in their ears, Virginia and the Duke raced neck to neck over the soft turf.

They must have ridden for nearly a mile and a half before the Duke reined in his horse. Virginia pulled up beside him and laughed happily as her eyes met his, her face glowing, her hair a little windswept, her eyes alight in the sunshine.

"That was wonderful!" she cried.

"It has cleared away the cobwebs, hasn't it?" he declared.

"What a perfect place for a gallop," Virginia said. "But you said no one comes here. Why?"

"I will show you," he answered.

After they had ridden side by side for a short distance, he pointed ahead.

"You see," he said.

"What is it?" Virginia asked, looking at a jagged cleft in the ground.

"It is an old tin mine," the Duke explained, "started by the Romans when they landed here and first began to build where the Castle now stands. It has been worked intermittently through the centuries but now it is derelict. It is very deep and very dangerous. That is why the farmers keep their cattle away from this part of the estate. The shepherds dread it, especially in the lambing season."

They drew a little nearer and Virginia looked down into the mine. It was dark and rather sinister and the edges had crumbled away. She could see that it would be a trap for anyone walking over the downs on a misty night or for an animal that had lost its way.

"You should fence it in," Virginia suggested.

The Duke laughed.

"There speaks the practical American! I do not suppose anyone round here has ever thought of such a thing. No, they just avoid it. Only I come this way to exercise my horses."

"And today I have come too," she said.

"Do you think I have forgotten that?" the Duke asked. "Look, Virginia, there is a little wood down there. Shall we go there so that we can talk?"

She knew it was not so much that he wanted to talk as to touch her. She, too, felt that all she wanted at that moment was the feel of his arms around her and his lips on hers. He did not have to hear the answer to his suggestion, he knew what she wanted by the sudden light in her eyes and quickening of her breath.

"There are things we must talk about," she said almost automatically.

"Yes, of course," he answered. "But it is difficult at the moment, Virginia, to think of anything but you."

She did not answer and after a moment he went on:

"I have never seen a girl ride as well as you. I thought it was only English women who looked right on a horse, but somehow you make them all look clumsy. One day I want to take you out hunting—not dressed like that, though! The Master would have a stroke! But I should like to see you take your fences . . ."

His voice ceased and Virginia wondered if he had suddenly realised how difficult it would be to introduce her to the hunt. How would he explain her presence? Then she put such thoughts from her. What did it matter what happened in the future so long as they were together now?

They were nearing the little wood when suddenly she looked down and saw, far below them, coming across the fields from the direction of the Castle, a lone rider. The Duke, who was looking at her, had not seen him.

"There is someone coming," she said.

She saw the look of irritation on his face as he followed the direction of her eyes. Then his sudden tension made her look again.

"It is Marcus," he said angrily.

"Did he know you were coming here?" Virginia asked.

"No! But you heard me say in the stable-yard where I was going."

"Do you think that he asked them?"

"I think," the Duke said slowly, "that he is looking for me."

"Oh, no! No!" Virginia cried. "Come away quickly. He will not have seen you. We are almost in the shadow of the trees."

"I do not want him to see you," the Duke replied. "That is what matters. He must not connect us. Virginia, go home. Follow the path through the wood. It will bring you out above the Castle gardens."

"And leave you here alone?" Virginia asked.

"I have to meet him sooner or later," the Duke answered, "and if he has come in search of me, it is obvious he has something to say."

"No, do not meet him! Not here!" Virginia pleaded.

"My dear, what can he do to me?" the Duke asked.

"The sword-stick!" she gasped.

"My horse is far swifter than his," the Duke said. "And I have a feeling that it would be very difficult to explain if I were found dead with Marcus's sword-stick through my chest."

"Sebastian, he is a desperate man!" Virginia warned.

"I do not intend to die yet," the Duke said. "Not until I have kissed you again!" He turned his horse. "Do as I tell you," he said in a voice of command. "I shall be angry, Virginia, if you do not obey me. I promise you I know what is best. Go now, at once."

There was something in his voice which made her feel she could not disobey. She moved into the shelter of the trees and then turned her horse to watch the Duke trot away from the wood. Whilst they had been talking Marcus had reached the flats and was moving at a tremendous pace. The Duke drew in his horse and stood waiting for him. He looked arrogant and supremely confident on his great black stallion, his head above his broad shoulders held imperiously high as if he defied the challenge any man might make to him.

"He is magnificent," Virginia whispered to herself, and turned her head to watch Marcus Ryll's approach.

It was then, through the branches of the trees which concealed her, she saw what he carried in his hand. It was the sword-stick and even as he galloped towards the Duke he drew it from its sheath. She wanted to scream out, to cry, to warn the Duke; but she knew that he too must have seen it and she saw that he was completely at ease astride his horse waiting for his cousin's approach.

"He will not dare," Virginia thought to herself. "He could not stab him now." Then as she waited for Marcus to draw alongside the Duke, watching him as if it were a picture moving before her eyes and not a reality, to her astonishment as he approached, still at a gallop, he veered to the back of the stallion and reached out.

Virginia stifled a scream, for it was not at the Duke that he lunged with his sword-stick but at the black stallion, piercing him in the hind-quarter and causing the wounded animal to rear high in the air, prancing and kicking in pain. Marcus turned his horse and galloped back. Now the Duke, fighting for the control of his mount, could do nothing to prevent him stabbing at the animal again, the sword-stick entering the shining flank to a depth of two or three inches and drawing a great spurt of blood.

Frantic with pain, the stallion began to gallop away from its adversary, with Marcus Ryll following, leaning far forward over his horse's neck to pierce the bleeding rear of the fleeing animal again and again. Then, with a horror almost beyond endurance, Virginia saw that Marcus was driving the black stallion towards the tin mine; driving him relentlessly with thrust after thrust of the sword-stick while the tortured creature reared and plunged.

Virginia heard a voice shouting furiously, but she could not be certain whether it was the Duke or Marcus who spoke; for the words were carried away on the wind. The two horses were drawing nearer and nearer to the mine and she could only wait and watch, her heart in her mouth.

Then, when she felt she must faint from the sheer terror of what was happening, she saw on the very edge of that gaping, dark place the Duke turn his horse at the last moment with a superb piece of riding. But Marcus Ryll, still at the gallop, his sword-stick pointed forward, did not realise until too late that he was outmanoeuvred.

With only one hand on the reins he had not the mastery over his animal that he should have had. Both horse and master saw the danger and in a wild, instinctive effort to avoid destruction, the horse jumped. For a second they were both silhouetted high in the air against the sky—then they were gone! Vanished from sight in an instant!

For Virginia everything seemed to go black. Her head fell forward and she knew that she was falling semi-conscious from the saddle. With an almost superhuman effort she pulled herself up and the breath that she had held for too long came gasping from her lips.

Her eyes were half closed yet she could see the Duke. He was standing at his horse's head, patting and soothing the frightened animal. Then he turned and leading the stallion by the bridle started to walk towards her and she knew that though the world itself came to an end all that mattered was that he was safe.

11

THE Castle seemed very empty. It was only six days since the Duke had gone north to Yorkshire with Marcus Ryll's coffin, but it seemed a lifetime to Virginia. She had not seen him since that moment when he had come to her amongst the trees and she had forced herself not to faint but to remain upright in the saddle.

There had seemed to be nothing for either of them to say; they could only look into each other's eyes and know they had passed through Hell. Virginia was trembling and the tears were running unchecked down her cheeks. Then abruptly the Duke said:

"Go back to the house."

With an effort she found her voice.

"Where . . . are you . . . going?"

"To fetch help," he answered. "No one must know that we were here together. I will not have you questioned. Tell them in the stables that you were tired and that I went on alone."

He had mounted and moved away almost before he finished speaking, and though he appeared self-controlled Virginia had known by the pallor of his face and the tension in his voice that he was in a state of deep shock. There was nothing else for her to do but obey him. Only after she had managed to speak quite casually to the grooms and had reached the sanctuary of her own bedroom, did she feel the whole horror of what had happened sweep over her. Standing in front of her mirror she was conscious of being terribly cold.

But the relief of knowing the Duke was at last free from danger gradually smoothed away the shock of Marcus Ryll's fall. Some hours later the Castle learned that he was dead, and Miss Marshbanks informed Virginia that his body was to be taken to Yorkshire where his mother lived and that the Duke would accompany it.

Now that there were no more duties to occupy her, Miss Marshbanks collapsed entirely. Despite her protestations Virginia insisted on sending for the doctor who said she must be kept quiet and stay in bed. What he did not prescribe was how to ease a broken heart, for the whole of Miss Marshbanks' life had been centred on the Duchess and now she no longer had anything to live for.

Virginia spent a lot of time by her bedside and Miss Marshbanks talked of the old days when she had first come to the Castle. She told of the great Balls at which the Duchess had been more beautiful than anyone else present. She talked of the dinner-parties where the Duchess was brilliant and vivacious. She told of how the Royal Family would come to stay, to dine or to shoot, and of the preparations that were made for them and what other guests were invited to meet them.

It was all like delving into the annals of the past and sometimes Virginia wished that she could write down all Miss Marshbanks told her; for she was certain that in the future it would have been a historical guide to the period. But there was one thing about which Miss Marshbanks never spoke and that was the secret errands on which the Duchess sent her to the village, and the reason why Her Grace had ordered Miss Marshbanks to collect certain letters from the postman before he delivered them at the Castle. These things were kept hidden, and although she chided herself for her curiosity Virginia could not help being curious about them.

The days seemed to stretch out endlessly. Virginia would ride alone in the morning and spend an hour or so with Miss Marshbanks. After luncheon, when Miss Marshbanks slept, she would wander round the state rooms of the Castle and try to learn something of the treasures that it contained.

Spread over more than four acres, the Castle was a living memorial to the past, and Virginia began to understand how much such a possession could come to mean. It could never belong to one person only but to a family, to each succeeding generation, and because it was so precious, those who held it in trust must try to leave it enriched.

Coming in from the gardens rather later than usual, Virginia thought ruefully that she had missed tea with Miss Marshbanks. She remembered that the tray was carried up to her room punctually at half past four; it was now after five. The time had slipped by because she had been wandering through the herb garden first planted in Elizabethan times and trying to discover, with the aid of an ancient book of recipes she had found in the still-room, exactly which herbs were used for which ailments.

It had been a fascinating study, but now she realised she should have been more punctilious and she hurried across the hall preparatory to running up to Miss Marshbanks' room.

"Excuse me, miss," a voice said behind her and she turned to see Matthews.

"Yes, Matthews?" she asked.

"There is a note, miss, from His Grace."

He held a silver salver towards her and Virginia felt her heart give a sudden leap of excitement.

"His Grace has returned?" she asked.

She had to force herself to speak calmly.

"Yes, indeed, miss! His Grace returned nearly half an hour ago," Matthews replied. "The agent was waiting to see him. I think His Grace has gone out with him."

"Thank you, Matthews," Virginia said, feeling breathless.

She went upstairs to her own room. She did not attempt to open the note until she had shut the door behind her. Then she stared for a moment at her name written in that strong, upright hand. She opened it with fingers which felt too clumsy to perform such a simple task. The note was very short.

My darling,
 Will you dine with me at eight o'clock? A carriage will be waiting for you at a quarter-to. You know that the one thing I want, above all else, is to see you again.
 Sebastian

Virginia realised that the Duke had signed his name and had headed his letter and she knew, because she loved him, that something new had happened between them.

She put down the note and after a moment or so went up to Miss Marshbanks' room. She knew it was unkind but she was glad that Miss Marshbanks was tired and did not want to talk. She was glad too, although she would not have admitted it, that Miss Marshbanks was ill and she would not have to explain what she was about to do this evening.

It took her a long time to dress. She wanted to look her very best and when, finally, she looked at herself in the mirror she knew she had succeeded. There was one gown she had brought with her from America—"Just in case," Aunt Ella May had said, "you are asked to a dance!" Virginia had known such a contingency was most unlikely, at the same time she could not resist buying just one really glamorous ball-gown. And tonight she could wear it!

It was very pale gold, almost the colour of her hair, and embroidered on to the skirt were tiny flecks of gold which glittered with every movement. Soft, glittering tulle formed small puff sleeves. There was a wide waistband of gold sequins to encircle her tiny waist and frills of tulle at the hem of her skirt, which stretched out behind her in a small train as she walked.

Virginia brushed her hair until it shone and then dressed it simply in a fashion she had made all her own. She half wished that she had a diamond necklace to clasp around her neck and did not realise that her eyes shone brighter than any jewels. Nevertheless, she would have been a fool if she had not realised when finally she was ready, that she looked very lovely.

There was an aura of excitement about her which made her seem to shimmer and glow. She felt as if the curtain were rising on a wonderful and thrilling play. There was just that same breathless sense of anticipation. She had wondered while she was dressing where they would be dining. It seemed strange that the Duke should take her out. Surely they were not going to a party with other people? She felt her spirits drop at the idea; then she thought, what did it matter where they went so long as they were together, so long as she would see him again?

She had known all this last week that things could not go on as they were. It was time for her to go back to America. Miss Marshbanks had arranged to stay with relations as soon as she was better, and that meant that Virginia could not stay on at the Castle alone with the Duke. Even though she knew she was considered of little consequence in the social scale, a young woman of her age staying alone with, and being constantly in the company of, a distinguished and married man would certainly cause a scandal.

But apart from this, she had told herself she must leave and, indeed, her clothes were already packed in the round-topped trunks with which she had arrived from America. She looked at them now, and the thought ran through her mind that perhaps after tonight she could unpack them again. Then, resolutely, she turned away and went downstairs.

It was a very warm, windless evening and although she

did not need a wrap she took with her a long, glittering scarf. There seemed no necessity to put it over her shoulders as she imagined the carriage would be closed. Matthews and three footmen were waiting for her in the hall. The old man looked impressive and she fancied there was an expression on the footmens' faces which suggested that something untoward was happening.

Then she stepped outside. For a moment she stared in amazement and then gave a cry of sheer delight. Waiting at the bottom of the steps was a small carriage such as a child might use. It was, in fact, a miniature Victoria, but so tiny that only one person could sit facing the horses and one back to them. Instead of the hood being up it was decorated with flowers—roses, carnations, stocks all scented the air from this tiny conveyance and it was drawn by three small, brown-and-white Shetland ponies.

Beside each pony was its groom, wearing the Duke's blue and white livery, with powdered wigs and peaked caps. The ponies tossed their heads, their silver harnesses jangled, ostrich feathers of red and white fluttered above their foreheads with the movement.

"Oh, how lovely!" Virginia cried.

"It has not been used for many years, miss," Matthews' respectful voice said beside her. "It was made, in fact, for Her Majesty Queen Victoria's first daughter, the Princess Royal, when she visited the Castle as a child. To my knowledge it has been used only two or three times since."

"It is exquisite!" Virginia exclaimed.

Matthews handed her in and she found, as she was so small, she could sit comfortably on the back seat. Anyone larger might have felt almost ridiculous, but as they moved off Virginia told herself she was like Cinderella. "I have my fairy coach," she said to herself, "and now I shall meet Prince Charming."

She wondered where they might be going and when they turned off the drive, down the small grass track, she knew where it would be—the temple on the lake! The place which the Duke had told her had been built by the same ancestor who had built Queen's Heart for the woman he loved.

The sun was sinking in a blaze of glory. In the east the sky was pale and translucent and there was no sign of darkness as Virginia alighted from her coach. They had circled the lake to where there was a small, Chinese bridge just like one on a willow-pattern plate, which she had never seen before and which spanned the water to reach the island.

Slowly, because she really longed to hurry, Virginia moved across it. At the other end there was a door into the Grecian temple which she had so often seen in the distance. A footman opened the door for her. She entered and gave a little gasp.

She had a quick impression of a rounded room, of blue curtains hanging from walls which rose to a domed ceiling. And then she saw nothing but flowers—flowers in garlands from the ceiling, great banks of lilies against the blue curtains, and an opening on to the terrace revealed flowers and more flowers.

Just for a moment her eyes took it all in, and then she saw only one person, someone who turned from the terrace where he had been looking down the lake. He was silhouetted against the sunset and it seemed to her that he came towards her in a burst of fire.

"Virginia!"

He had only to say her name to make her feel as if he told her all that was in both their hearts, and then he lifted her hands to his lips and she felt the warm, hungry possessiveness of his mouth on her skin.

"Let me look at you!"

Still holding her hands he opened her arms wide and stood back so that he could look down at her.

"You look like a ray of sunshine!" he said. "No, a star that has fallen out of the sky. The star that shall guide, inspire and help me. Is that what you are, Virginia? My star?"

"You have . . . come back," she said, because she could think of nothing to say except what was most important.

"I have come back—to you," he said softly. "Come, let us have dinner."

He took her by the hand and led her out on to the terrace. It was little more than a large balcony perched on the edge of the island, concealed from the Castle by trees and shrubs but affording a perfect view down the lake to where, in the distance, there was a bridge, and beyond it the stream, winding its way through the green park.

On the terrace there was a table laid for two, decorated with orchids and smilax. The balustrade was bordered in flowers, mostly lilies, which Virginia loved and which gave the air a heavy, exotic fragrance.

"Have you missed me?" the Duke asked.

The light of the setting sun was full on his face, and looking at him Virginia realised something had happened. He had changed. Gone were the cynical, hard, tense lines which had made him seem so frightening. Gone was the tight-lipped reserve and that air of eternally battling against something unknown. He looked, for the first time since she had known him, young and carefree, and she knew she had been right in thinking that something had happened which might alter their entire relationship to each other.

Because she was shy she could not meet his eyes.

"I think you are fishing for compliments," she replied in answer to his question.

"Are you flirting with me, Virginia?" he asked, and there was a smile at the corners of his lips. "It is something you have never done before."

Virginia laughed. "There never seemed to be the opportunity," she confessed. "We have always seemed to be involved in serious, frightening events."

"And now all the dragons have been vanquished," he said. "Not by St. George—he cannot claim the credit—but by his princess. My lucky star! Do you realise, Virginia, that if it were not for you I should be dead?"

Virginia gave a little shudder.

"Do not let us speak of it," she begged. "Not tonight. Let us forget it all happened. Let us pretend that we have not passed through all those terrible things together. They never happened. Instead, we are just two people who have met, two people who ... like each other ... a little."

"Who love each other, Virginia!" the Duke corrected. "Let us be truthful. I love you and I am no longer afraid to say so. I love you, Virginia!"

She felt herself quiver and tingle from the passion in his voice.

He led her to the table. The footmen brought delicious, exotic dishes; they poured wine into the crystal goblets. But Virginia had no idea what she ate or drank. She only knew time passed quickly and then, as darkness fell, Virginia looked out at the lake and saw that all along its banks there were twinkling lights. Unseen hands lit them and unseen hands pushed them out on to the still water, tiny ships fashioned of flowers in the centre of which glowed a flickering candle.

"How pretty! How could you think of anything so pretty?" Virginia asked.

They rose from the table to look and when they turned

back again the table had vanished and so had the servants. There was only a soft-cushioned, comfortable sofa on which she could sit beside the Duke and look out over the lake. He sat down and took her hand in his.

"Has this made you happy?" he asked. "Your eyes are shining more brightly than any light that could glow on the lake."

"You know I am happy," Virginia answered. "Not only because you have done all this for me but because we are together. It was stupid of me, but I felt when you went away that I would never see you again. Even now I cannot believe that there is not danger lurking in every shadow or that I need not be afraid of everything you eat and every step you take."

"Did you really feel like that for me?" the Duke asked.

"If I were flirting with you," Virginia replied, "I should not say so. But . . . yes—that is what I felt!"

"My darling, how can I ever tell you what this means to me?" the Duke said. "I want to tell you something. All my life I have wanted someone to love me for myself—not because I was a Duke, rich, powerful, important, but because I was just a man."

He paused for a moment looking away, and Virginia knew memories from the past were hurting him.

"When I was very young," he went on in a low voice, "I fell in love with a very beautiful girl who I thought loved me as much as I loved her. She told me she did. She said nothing mattered except that I was myself. We were engaged to be married and then one day, quite by chance, I found out she was really in love with a man who was poor. She would not share his life because she wanted all the things that I could give her because I was my father's son."

Virginia gave a little exclamation of sympathy. The Duke's fingers tightened on hers.

"It seems silly now," the Duke said, "to remember how much I suffered. The young are very vulnerable. What I learned made me grow up overnight and also made me very cynical where women are concerned. I have had many love affairs, Virginia, I am not seeking to conceal it. If women were prepared to offer me their favours I should have been inhuman had I refused them. But all the same, at the back of my mind there was always the doubt whether they would have been so generous if I had not been of such social consequence. It has poisoned my whole life. Always I have been seeking someone who would love me; who had nothing to gain from an association with me—nothing except love."

"I suppose that is what we all seek," Virginia said in a soft voice.

"And you, Virginia, what do you want?" the Duke asked.

"Every woman wants to be loved for herself," Virginia answered slowly. "But most of all, she wants to feel that she matters more than anything else in a man's life. She wants to be first. She wants to be all-important."

She raised her eyes to his and the Duke said inconsequentially:

"I have never seen a woman's face that changed as yours does. When you are serious your eyes seem to darken and when you are gay and laughing they light up. Oh, my sweet, you are so beautiful and you are so different from anyone I have ever known before."

"Why do you say that?" Virginia asked.

"I suppose in some ways it is because you are an American," the Duke said. "You are not tied by convention, caste-bound, tyrannised over by social protocol. But those things are unimportant. It is what you are yourself. You are so straight and forthright. In some ways you are almost unfeminine in your frankness, in your honesty, and yet, at the same time, you are all woman. Tell me, Virginia, how much do we really mean to each other?"

Virginia rose to her feet and walked to the edge of the terrace.

"I cannot answer that," she said, "not where you are concerned. Our lives have been so very different."

"They have been different," the Duke agreed, "and yet I think we bridged the gulf the first time we looked into each other's eyes. Does anything matter except us, Virginia?"

She turned round to face him.

"Only you can answer that," she said.

He did not look at her but walked to the other end of the terrace; his hands clasped the balustrade and she saw that his knuckles were white. "Isn't love enough?" he asked hoarsely.

"I think," Virginia replied, "it depends on what you mean by love."

He turned round and without warning took her in his arms.

"I love you," he said. "God! How much I love you!"

His lips found her mouth and for a moment they united

in a kiss which made them not man and woman but one person. Virginia felt as if her whole body surrendered to him, that the world slipped away and they were alone, caught between heaven and earth, two hearts joined because they had searched for each other through eternity and were at last together.

"I love you," the Duke murmured and his voice was deep with passion.

He kissed her cheeks, her eyes, her hair and then her neck where a little pulse was beating with excitement and happiness. He kissed her shoulders and the whiteness of her skin above her breasts, and then her lips again.

"Oh, Virginia! Virginia!"

He seemed to be calling her from a far distance and she felt herself thrill and quiver with an ecstasy she had never known was possible. She was like a musical instrument vibrating at the touch of his hands. She felt as if his lips drew her very soul from her body and took it into his keeping.

How long they stood locked together she had no idea, and then, suddenly, she was free.

"I have something to show you," the Duke said.

He took her by the hand and led her from the terrace back into the rounded room of the temple. The curtains had been drawn over the entrance and they stepped through them into a strange enchantment. Other curtains had been caught back to reveal an alcove directly facing the terrace from which they had entered. In it stood a bed.

It was the most amazing bed Virginia had ever seen. It was canopied and carved with a hundred small, pink, white and gilt cupids. There were cupids hanging from the ceiling, each holding a lighted candle in its tiny hand and cupids seemed to fly through the air towards the great bed which was surrounded by entwined hearts. The scent of lilies, the soft light of the candles and an atmosphere of beauty, love and passion seemed to pervade everything.

For a moment Virginia stood very still and then she turned to look at the Duke. He was no longer touching her but standing a little aside, his eyes on her face.

"I told you," he said very quietly, "that this was the temple of love. My ancestor who built it and brought all these things from Austria did it for someone he loved beyond life itself. They were very happy, those two lovers of the past—very happy, Virginia."

He paused, then went on:

"Outside your carriage is waiting. I would not plead with you, I would not dissuade you in any way from leaving now and going back to the Castle. I would only tell you, as I have already told you, I love you with all my heart. I can offer you nothing, for I have nothing to offer except my heart. It is yours, Virginia, to do with as you wish. I have only that—to lay at your feet."

There was silence. The Duke's voice seemed to echo round the scented room. Virginia was very still. It seemed to her that even the candles were no longer flickering. Everything was waiting . . . waiting for her answer.

Then, as if the strain was too much, the Duke said harshly:

"If you must go, go quickly, Virginia, or I might not be able to let you. I love and worship you, but I am also a man and I desire you utterly. I want you! My whole body aches for you! I want you as no man ever wanted a woman before . . ."

His voice died away. Virginia saw the expression on his face and knew that he was almost at breaking-point. Suddenly she knew what she must do. She did not move, she only said very, very softly:

"I love you . . . as a . . . a man, Sebastian!"

With a cry of inarticulate triumph the Duke caught her in his arms, lifted her high against his heart and carried her towards the great bed.

12

AUNT ELLA MAY, rolling the pastry in her farm kitchen, looked through the window to see Virginia walking up the dusty drive. She gave a little sigh and rolled her pastry with an extra strength as if to relieve her feelings, for she knew by the way Virginia walked, by the sag of her shoulders, by her bent head, that there had been nothing in the post-box.

Twice a day since her return Virginia had walked to the post-box which stood on the main road, but always she had come back empty-handed. Unable to concentrate on her cooking, Aunt Ella May looked up several times as Virginia neared the house and saw her turn from the door to enter the garden.

On an impulse Aunt Ella May walked from the kitchen,

through the house and on to the wide wooden verandah. Virginia was in the flower-garden and she looked a little like a flower herself with the sun shining on the pale gold of her hair.

"Drat the man!" Aunt Ella May murmured beneath her breath. She wanted to go to Virginia, put her arms around her and try to protect her against the unhappiness which was tearing her in pieces. But she knew, despairingly, there was nothing more she could do—nothing which she had not done already.

When Virginia had arrived back over a week before, pale and wan and looking as if she had not slept for nights, Aunt Ella May had taken her in her arms. But her love seemed unable to warm something that was frozen. It had not taken long, however, for Virginia to break down and talk.

Virginia had told Aunt Ella May how she had arrived in England hating the Duke, and shocked by her first sight of him storming on the Castle steps. Then, as she went on to speak of him, her face came alive and her voice was deep and passionate. Her eyes shone. Long before she actually said the words, "I fell in love with him," Aunt Ella May knew the truth.

They had sat up far into the night, Virginia talking as if the restraint of the dreary days at sea had been almost impossible to bear. She told Aunt Ella May of the strange, unaccountable behaviour of the Duchess, of the plots against the Duke and her own reaction to the treachery of his cousin. It was as if, in recounting to her aunt what had happened, she re-created every moment that she had spent in England. When she related how, after the Duchess's pug had died from taking the poison, the Duke had drawn her into the *boudior* and taken her into his arms, she sat for a moment in silence, her eyes wide, her lips parted as, once again, she lived through the ecstasy and rapture of that moment.

"If you realised then that he loved you," Aunt Ella May said gently, "why did you not tell him who you were?"

"I knew that he loved me," Virginia answered, "but only in his own way. He loved me as any man might love an attractive woman."

She went on then to speak of Queen's Heart and, finally, she came to that last night. The night when, young, carefree and quite different from the man she had known before, he had given her dinner on the terrace outside the little temple dedicated to love; and then, as the lights on the lake flickered away into the darkness, he had drawn her inside the room with its cupids, its garlands of flowers and its great, carved bed.

It was now that Virginia's story came in hesitating, broken sentences and Aunt Ella May filled in for herself the wonder of the moment when the Duke had asked Virginia to love him as a man and challenged her to prove that her love for him asked for nothing else.

"The carriage . . . was . . . was waiting," Virginia stammered, "but . . . I could . . . not leave."

"And yet you came away?" Aunt Ella May said softly.

"Yes, I . . . came . . . away," Virginia answered. "I knew it was . . . nearly dawn. There was a faint light coming through the curtains and I could hear the birds stirring."

"You did not say anything to him?" Aunt Ella May inquired.

"He was asleep," Virginia said. "The candles had gone out. In the darkness I knew he was looking young, happy and relaxed as I had never seen him before. I slipped from his side, dressed and went from the room. He . . . he never heard me go."

"How could you have left him?" Aunt Ella May asked.

"I . . . had to," Virginia said. "I had to come back here and . . . wait."

"What for? I do not understand," Aunt Ella May insisted. "You are his wife. He loves you and you love him."

"He does not know I am his wife," Virginia said. "And I cannot know if . . . if he loves me as I love him."

"What do you mean by that?" Aunt Ella May demanded.

Virginia had risen to her feet to walk restlessly across the room and back again.

"Ever since I arrived at the Castle I was told that one thing mattered more than anything else," she said. "Miss Marshbanks told me, and Sebastian himself said it, not once but several times. 'There must be no scandal.' That sums up the whole code of behaviour for the family, for their retainers, for the society in which they live: there must be no scandal. They will sacrifice anything for that. They will torture themselves, they will deprive themselves, they will, I think, even die so that the family honour shall remain unbesmirched, untarnished. Standing on the terrace at Queen's Heart Sebastian said, 'We have never had a divorce in our family.' "

"I still do not understand," Aunt Ella May complained.

"But do you not see?" Virginia asked almost fiercely. "He loves an unknown, unimportant American girl. The question is, does he love her enough to make her his wife?"

"You mean," Aunt Ella May said almost in shocked tones, "that you want to force him into asking for a divorce so that he may marry you?"

Virginia gave a little cry and covered her face with her hands.

"Can you not understand?" she said. "If I went to him now and told him who I was, I should never believe that his love was as great as mine. I should never know that he was not still wanting me for my money rather than myself! Oh, I know that for the moment he is in love with a pretty face. When he is with me I feel as if we were part of each other, meant to belong since the beginning of time. And yet some vital part of my mind is not satisfied. He married a woman for her money. He was mean with his mother although he had all that wealth at his finger-tips. Do you really believe that he would make a sacrifice of millions and millions of dollars for a woman of whom he really knows nothing—except that she inflames and excites him?"

Aunt Ella May gave a deep sigh.

"I know the English," she said. "The honour of their family means more to them than to any other people in the world. Are you wise to ask so much, Virginia? Can you not be satisfied that by what is almost a miracle you have fallen in love with your own husband and he with you?"

"How could I live with him and be tortured day after day and night after night with the thought that the only thing he wanted of me was my body?" Virginia answered. "I gave him that willingly. I surrendered myself because I loved him and because every nerve in me vibrated to him and his need of me. But my love for him is deeper than that and I cannot be satisfied with second best."

Aunt Ella May clasped her hands together.

"Oh, my dear!" she wailed. "You are gambling with hearts! You are asking a very great deal—perhaps more than you realise. Everything that your husband is today is part of the society in which he has been bred and brought up. It has been ingrained in him since he was a tiny child that he personally is but one link in a long chain of Rylls stretching back in history. He has been taught that his ancestors made sacrifices for what they believed was right. They went to wars when they could have stayed at home; they made marriages so that estates could be merged. Their whole object was to ensure the continuity of the family, and anyone who disobeyed the strict code they had set for themselves was not only wrong or wicked but a traitor to all they held sacred."

"I know all this," Virginia said passionately. "Do you think I did not find it on every page of the family history? I saw it in the faces of Sebastian's ancestors looking down at me from the portraits in the picture gallery and on the stairs. Perhaps you are right! Perhaps the family means more to Sebastian than anything else—in which case, when he comes here in search of me, tell him that I am dead, for my heart will have died!"

"You cannot expect me to say that," Aunt Ella May protested.

"It would be true," Virginia retorted, "for without him I no longer want to live. If this is what you brought me back to life for, Aunt Ella May, then I only wish you had left me to die!"

Aunt Ella May knew in the days that followed how desperately Virginia was suffering. She would eat little and her aunt would find her wandering about her room late at night or coming downstairs when the dawn was breaking, to sit on a rocking-chair on the verandah looking out over the garden, across the fields to the woods.

It seemed that only in the woods, under the cool, green branches that were a protection against the midday sun, did she find any comfort, and Aunt Ella May guessed that in some way they reminded her of the woods in England.

Watching Virginia now, moving across the garden, Aunt Ella May knew she had grown much thinner since she returned. Already she was beginning to see again that skeleton of a girl who had lain, month after month, at the farm, neither alive nor dead but in a twilight world where no one could reach her.

"Drat the man!" Aunt Ella May said again and returned through the house to the kitchen.

It was as she picked up the rolling-pin to continue her task that she heard the sound of horses coming up the drive. She looked out to see a carriage drawn by two horses travelling swiftly and putting up a fine dust as they did so.

Hastily Aunt Ella May took off her apron and instinctively her hand went to her head to tidy her hair. Then, with her lips tight set and her eyes a little wary, she went to the front door and opened it just as the Duke stepped out of the carriage.

He looked at Aunt Ella May for a moment in an uncertain fashion as if he was not sure if he recognised her. Then he smiled and held out his hand.

"It is a long time since we met," he said.

"How do you do," Aunt Ella May replied a little stiffly. "Will you come in?"

She led the way through the cool hall into the sitting-room, with its wooden beams, the big, open fireplace where in the winter logs burned, its comfortable sofas and large, man-sized armchairs.

"Please sit down," Aunt Ella May suggested. "May I offer you some refreshment?"

"Thank you, I want nothing," the Duke answered, "except to talk to you."

He spoke almost impatiently, as if he were anxious not to waste any time, and Aunt Ella May glanced at him speculatively as she took a seat opposite him. He looked amazingly handsome, she thought, but thin and a little drawn. There was something about him which gave her the impression that he was a man who had driven himself almost beyond endurance.

"I expect you are surprised to see me," the Duke began. "I should have let you know of my arrival, but I left England in a great hurry."

"You know you are welcome at any time," Aunt Ella May said quietly.

"I would have been here sooner," the Duke went on as if she had not spoken, "but I stopped in New York to call at the Chase Bank. They are, as of course you know, the bankers to . . . my wife!" There was just a pause before he said the last two words.

"Yes, that is right," Aunt Ella May agreed.

"I wished to see the manager in person," the Duke went on, "and I placed in his safe keeping the sum of four hundred thousand pounds—in your currency, two million dollars."

There was a little pause before Aunt Ella May asked:

"May I ask why you felt impelled to do this?"

For the first time a faint smile touched the Duke's lips.

"It is something I would have done far sooner had it

been possible," he replied. "May I give you an explanation? It is what I have come here to do."

"Yes, of course," Aunt Ella May said, her eyes on his face.

"Out of all the people who surged around me on my last visit to New York," the Duke began, "you were the only person I can remember clearly. When everything seemed to happen at once—when my wife collapsed and, later, Mrs. Clay had a stroke—you were so calm and clear-headed and helpful that you have always seemed to me the one person to whom I should explain what has happened."

"I should be glad to listen," Aunt Ella May said.

"That is what I hoped you would say," the Duke answered, "and so, if I may, I will start at the very beginning."

He paused for a moment as if he were choosing his words and then continued:

"My father was a very fine person. Everybody admired and respected him and he was my hero since I was a small boy. I loved my mother; she was beautiful and to me she always seemed like some enchanted princess, but as I grew older I realised that she worried my father a great deal and although he loved her he was frequently very angry with her."

The Duke glanced towards Aunt Ella May and said:

"Of course, I am telling you all this in confidence. I need not say that, need I?"

"Of course not," Aunt Ella May agreed.

"I suppose I must have been fourteen or fifteen years old," the Duke went on, "before I understood what annoyed my father. It was my mother's incessant gambling. It was in her blood, she could not help it. She was really only happy when she had a pack of cards in her hand; every day of her life she wanted to place a dozen bets on the races and every night her eyes would light up after dinner when there was a chance of sitting down at the card table or playing roulette, *chemin de fer,* or any other gambling attraction that she could find.

"I learned later—I cannot now remember how but I expect it was through the servants—that my father had paid up her debts not once but a dozen times. On every such occasion she promised him faithfully that she would not gamble again except in very small sums, but always she broke her word and each time it happened it made him more and more distressed.

"Finally, two years ago my father became very ill and the doctors said that any excitement, any shock, anything that upset him in any way, might prove fatal. It was then that my mother started to conceal her gambling activities from him. She loved him and wanted him to be happy, so she never told him what was actually occurring until it was too late."

The Duke took a deep breath and rose to his feet. His voice, as he was talking, was very low and, in a way, quite unemotional. Aunt Ella May, looking at him, knew that this confession involved all the pain of a reserved man having to speak of intimate things which he would have preferred to keep to himself.

"In the spring last year my mother came to me in a really desperate state," the Duke went on. "She told me that she was in grave financial difficulty and she could not, she dared not, go to my father for help. She was so distressed that at first all I wanted to do was to comfort her, to assure her that I would help and that there was no reason to worry my father. Then, when I learned of the extent to which she was in debt, I was appalled."

The Duke looked at Aunt Ella May and said in a voice that was suddenly bitter:

"I think you can guess already how much my mother owed—half a million pounds! As you know, at the time my father was still alive and I had, in actual fact, very little money of my own. I knew at once that even if I sold everything I possessed it would not begin to realise the amount required, and even if I had gone to the moneylenders it would have been useless; for they would not have accepted my security in the matter unless it had been guaranteed by my father."

The Duke walked across the room and back again.

"My mother had the solution," he said, and his voice was hard. "She had, it appeared, been in touch with Mrs. Stuyvesant Clay for many years, and Mrs. Clay who had a marriageable daughter would be prepared to find that exact sum of money should I agree to marry the girl."

The Duke walked to the window and stood with his back to Aunt Ella May.

"I know exactly what you must have thought of me," he said, "and even now, I can see that I appear only a cad, a man who was making use of a woman entirely for his own ends. I cannot expect you to understand that at that moment there was nothing else I could do except risk killing my father.

"I came to America hating the part I must play in this despicable drama and determined that I would tell my bride, before I married her, the truth about why I was making this offer for her hand. You know that that proved impossible owing to the fact that the ship was so late in docking in New York harbour. I will also be honest with you and say that whilst I despised myself, I also despised the girl who was ready to sell herself in such a manner so that she might receive my title. I thought, as a matter of fact, that we were pretty much of a pair!"

The Duke paused and came back again to sit down opposite Aunt Ella May.

"Then," he went on, "I saw that poor, unhappy creature and I realised that what had happened had been none of her own choosing. I only had to speak to Mrs. Clay to know who was the driving force behind the whole scheme."

The Duke put up his hand to his eyes for a moment as if he would shut out the memory of the wedding, the scene of the bride's collapse, of the strident, commanding tones of Mrs. Clay's voice and the curiosity of the bystanders.

"You were the only person," he continued, "who seemed sane, calm and normal. I may be maligning them all, but I want to thank you, now, for taking my wife away from that bedlam. I only hope she is as grateful to you as I am."

"She is, indeed," Aunt Ella May declared.

"And now," the Duke said with what was clearly an effort, "we come to the point of why I am here. In your last letter—I brought it with me when I left home and I read it many times on the ship—you told me that my wife was much better and that the doctor was pleased with her progress. Is she well enough for me to see her?"

"Yes, I think she would be well enough to see you," Aunt Ella May said.

The Duke rose.

"Then may I see her?" he asked. "And alone!"

Aunt Ella May got to her feet almost as if she were surprised that her interview with the Duke had come to an end.

"If you will wait here," she said, "I will talk to her."

She went from the room. The Duke walked restlessly backwards and forwards on the soft rugs. He must have waited nearly ten minutes before the door opened. He did not know that Virginia had been on the verandah from the very moment of his arrival. He did not know that she had stood outside the door fighting for composure or that Aunt Ella May, after one glance at her on leaving the sitting-room, had walked past her without saying a word.

Softly the door opened and Virginia came into the room. It was almost as if she brought the sunshine with her; at the same time her eyes were dark and a little apprehensive.

The Duke, who had been moving across the floor, stopped suddenly.

"Virginia!"

The word seemed almost to break from his lips as the sound of a wave breaking against the rocks. Then they both stood transfixed looking at each other, neither of them, for the moment, capable of moving. After a very long pause the Duke said:

"Why are you here? I did not expect to see you! But, oh, Virginia! How could you have run away like that? You have tortured me! You have driven me mad! I have wondered every moment where you might be. I have thought of you in London, in the country, I even imagined you might have come back to America. Yet I could not come in search of you."

"Why not?" Virginia asked.

"How could you do this to me?" the Duke asked. "I have imagined you alone and frightened; I have thought of men being attracted to you; of you not having enough money. Oh, I cannot describe to you the fears that have tortured me! Why did you leave me?"

"Why are you here?" Virginia asked.

"I am here to see my wife," the Duke answered. "I have to see her. I had to see her before I could seek you. Go away! Do not distract me. I cannot talk to you and not want to take you in my arms. I want to touch you, to kiss you. Can you not realise that it is agony to look at you like this?"

Virginia's eyes were shining and for a moment it seemed as if she must put out her hands towards the Duke. Then she turned her face away.

"I do not think I understand," she whispered.

"You will never know what I suffered when I awoke to find you gone," the Duke said, almost as if he were speaking to himself. "I was frantic, I was desperate! I tore back to the Castle and they told me you had left. I felt like a madman."

"I . . . had to . . . go," Virginia murmured.

"Why did you have to leave me?" he demanded. "Had I disappointed you? I cannot believe it was that."

"You know it was not . . . that," Virginia said, and her voice deepened.

"Perhaps no man could have such happiness and then not be cast into Hell," the Duke said. "If you had hated me, Virginia, you could not have subjected me to more pain or agony of mind than I have been through these past two weeks. Can you imagine what it was like to cross the Atlantic thinking I was leaving you behind? Thinking that perhaps you were waiting for me somewhere in England and puzzled because I did not find you?"

"And yet you came here," Virginia said softly.

"As I have told you, I came to see my wife," the Duke said. As he spoke he moved across the room and stood close to her. "Why must you tempt me?" he asked. "I am trying to behave honourably; I am trying to do what is right. But when you look at me like that I forget everything except that you are here, except that once you told me that you loved me and gave yourself to me."

She looked up into his eyes. It seemed as if the world stood still. He did not touch her; instead he turned away roughly as if his iron control was near to breaking.

"Go away, Virginia!" he said harshly. "Ask your aunt to send my wife to me. I must speak to her first."

"What do you want of her?" Virginia asked.

"Do you not know?" the Duke replied. "Can you not guess? I have come here to ask my wife, on my knees if necessary, to divorce me. Now go, Virginia, and let me get on with what I have come to do."

"And supposing she refuses?" Virginia inquired.

"She cannot, she must not," the Duke said quietly. "I have to be free, and you know why."

There was a sudden tension in the room as Virginia said, almost as if she had deliberated her words for a long time:

"And if your wife refuses, would our love not be enough?"

"Enough?" the Duke asked sharply. "Enough for you or enough for me? You know, Virginia, it is not like that between us. You showed me all too clearly that day at Queen's Heart what you thought of a love which must be concealed, which must hide in corners. I want you as a woman—God knows, I want you like that—but I also want you as my wife, as the mother of my children, and that is why I must see my wife. I must throw myself on her mercy and beg her to release me from this marriage that is nothing but a mockery."

There was a sudden silence and Virginia clasped her hands together as if she would stop the trembling of her whole body. For a moment she felt as if she must faint at the very ecstasy of the joy that shot through her like a flame. Then, in a voice which trembled, she said:

"Sebastian, I have something to tell you."

"Go, Virginia!" he said almost angrily. "I can bear no more."

"But this is important, Sebastian! You must listen to me."

"What is it?" he asked, not looking at her.

"I am afraid that you will be angry with me," Virginia said. "I am afraid, Sebastian."

"Of me?" he questioned.

"Yes, you! When . . . you are . . . angry you do not . . . realise how . . . frightening you . . . can be."

He smiled as if he could not help it.

"Oh, Virginia," he said. "What a child you are! It is one of your most entrancing qualities, that you can turn from being a very serious young woman into a child who draws at one's heart-strings. Tell me what you have to say, Virginia. I will not be angry."

"You promise . . . whatever it might be?"

"I cannot imagine myself being angry with you," he said, "but if it gives you any pleasure, I promise."

"Then, Sebastian," Virginia said, and her voice was so low he could hardly hear the words, "Will you ask the question . . . that you came here to ask . . . if necessary on your . . . knees?"

"I do not understand what you are saying," the Duke said.

"You see . . . Sebastian . . ." Virginia faltered. "You have often said that . . . that I seemed so . . . honest and so . . . frank, but . . . but I was in fact . . . deceiving you."

"What are you talking about?" the Duke demanded roughly. "Deceiving me! With whom? There is not, there cannot be another man in your life."

He seized her by her arms so fiercely that his fingers bit into the softness of her skin.

"The only man in my life," Virginia whispered, "is . . . you . . . my . . . husband!"

For a moment the Duke stared at her as if she had taken

leave of her senses. Slowly his hands freed her. He stepped back, his face very pale.

"Are you trying to tell me," he asked, and his voice seemed strangled in his throat, "that you are my wife?"

"That is . . . right," Virginia said. "Oh, Sebastian, you promised not . . . to be . . . angry."

"I do not know what I feel," the Duke said. "I never dreamed of such a thing. But my wife was . . ."

"Fat and terrible to look at!" Virginia interrupted. "But she was still me. I could not help being like that. I had been fed wrongly. My mother thought that by stuffing me with every sort of delicacy she was making me strong, instead of which she was destroying me. I know what I looked like and that is why I knew you would not recognise me."

"So you came to England to spy on me!" the Duke said and his tone was harsh.

"Not at all," Virginia retorted. "I came to England because I . . . I hated you, because I despised you, because I . . . wanted a . . . divorce."

"You wanted a divorce!" the Duke repeated incredulously.

"Do you think I wanted to marry you?" Virginia asked. "I loathed and destested the idea, but my mother forced me to agree to it. I either had to marry you or spend seven years of my life in a House of Correction."

"I cannot believe it," the Duke exclaimed.

"My mother was a snob," Virginia replied. "She wanted so much for her daughter to be a Duchess, and she would stop at nothing to get her own way."

"I never thought of it being like that," the Duke said.

"And when I got better, when Aunt Ella May saved me from dying or going into a madhouse," Virginia went on, "I wanted only to be free of you. But she would not allow me to ask for my freedom unless I went to England and saw you for myself. And so I arrived at the Castle prepared to hate you. When I saw you throwing out those jewellers, swearing and cursing, you seemed just the type of man I expected I had married."

"So that was the first time you saw me," the Duke said. "I remember the incident only too well. My mother . . . it is a long story and I will explain it to you later, but she had sold some of the family heirlooms before. I had been forced to buy them back and those men had come back for more."

"Then, as you remember," Virginia continued, "we talked in the glade down by the lake and you were quite different from what I expected."

"And you saved my life," the Duke said softly.

"It was, perhaps, a good thing that I did go to England," Virginia smiled.

"You are my wife!" the Duke murmured. "I cannot believe it. I cannot take it in. I cannot imagine how you can look like you do instead of that . . ."

"Fat little dumpling with that terrible, vulgar tiara on my head," Virginia interposed.

"That poor little fat girl," the Duke corrected, "who I thought wanted my title."

He put his hand up to his eyes.

"I believe I am dreaming this," he said, "or is this, indeed, part of your deceits, Virginia?"

"Have you forgiven me?" Virginia asked.

"I should like to know one thing," the Duke said. "What do you think of me now—this man you despised, you hated, the fortune-hunter who came to America to get your money?"

He took a step nearer to Virginia as he spoke. She could not look at him and her lashes lay, long and dark, against her cheeks.

"I think you are proud . . . autocratic and sometimes overbearing and . . . masterful," she whispered, "but . . . very much . . . a man."

At the word which had meant so much to them the colour rose in her cheeks. The Duke was very near.

"You are right, Virginia," he said. "I am masterful."

He put his arms around her and drew her close against him.

"You are my wife," he said, "and let me make one thing very clear. There will never ever be a divorce, between us. So for as long as we live you will never escape me another time. In fact, I will never let you out of my sight. You are mine! Do you understand, Virginia? Mine! Not only because we are married but because you gave yourself to me."

He held her so closely that she felt unable to breathe. Then, as she could not look at him, he put his hand under her chin and turned her face up to his.

"Are you still afraid of me?" he asked. "For I promise you I shall be a very overbearing, autocratic husband. At the same time, Virginia, I shall love you utterly and completely, as no woman has ever been loved before. Tell me—tell me truthfully, is that what you want of me?"

She looked into his eyes and saw the passion burning there and knew that the flame in him was matched by a flame of desire rising in herself. Instinctively her arms went round his neck to draw his face down to hers.

"I love you, Sebastian," she whispered. "I love you as ... a man!"

Then, with his lips against hers, he murmured hoarsely:

"I love you, my darling, my sweet, my woman—and my wife!"